KISSES AND CHRISTMAS BELLS

ANNA CAMPBELL

Serenade Publishing

Publisher's Note: This is a work of fiction. Names, characters, places, and incidents are a product of the author's imagination. Locales and public names are sometimes used for atmospheric purposes. Any resemblance to actual people, living or dead, or to businesses, companies, events, institutions, or locales is completely coincidental.

ISBN: 978-1-925980-92-9

Cover design: By Hang Le

Print editions published by Serenade Publishing
www.serenadepublishing.com

MISTLETOE AND THE MAJOR

The Major is home from the wars at last...

Edmund Sherritt, Major Lord Canforth, has devoted eight tumultuous years to fighting Napoleon. Finally Europe is at peace, and he can retire to his estates and the lovely wife he hasn't seen since their brief, unhappy honeymoon. The innocent girl he loved from the first moment he saw her, but who shied away from him on their wedding night.

The beautiful woman who greets him at Otway Hall on Christmas Eve is no longer the sweet ingénue he remembers. This new and exciting version of his beloved countess is strong, outspoken, and independent, and she's willing to stand up for what she wants. The question is—does she want the husband who returns to her arms more as a stranger than a spouse?

Now the real battle begins.

Felicity, Lady Canforth, has had eight long years to regret that she sent her husband from a cold marriage bed to face brutal combat, danger and hardship. The only child of elderly parents, Felicity came to marriage innocent and ignorant, and unable to conceal her shock at the sensual power of the earl's caresses. Before she found the nerve to offer Canforth a more generous welcome, he was called away to war. The Major left behind a countess who was a bride, not a wife; a woman unsure of her husband's feelings, and too timid to confess how fervently she desires the man she wed.

Fate has granted an older, wiser Felicity a second chance to win her husband's heart. Now nothing will stop her from claiming victory over the famous war hero. This Christmas, she'll deploy every ounce of courage, purpose and passion to seize the life and love she's longed for, ever since Canforth left to serve his country. Whatever it costs, whatever it takes, she'll lure the dashing Major back into her bed, where she means to show him he's the only man she wants as her lover—and her love.

After years of yearning and separation, will a Christmas miracle heal the wounds of the past and offer the earl and his bride a future bright with love?

A MATCH MADE IN MISTLETOE

A mistletoe wish...

All her life, Serena Talbot has been in love with the handsome boy next door, Sir Paul Garside. She always eagerly looks forward to Paul's visit to her family over the Festive Season, even if he usually brings along his dark, sardonic friend Lord Hallam. This year, Serena is determined that Paul's kiss under the mistletoe will lead to a proposal. Even if she has to enlist every ounce of Christmas magic she can get her hands on to make that happen.

But the mistletoe gets it wrong!

When Serena slips a sprig of mistletoe from the village kissing bough under her pillow, it's not Paul who turns up in her dreams as the man she's going to marry, but brooding, intense, annoying Giles Farraday, Marquess of Hallam. Still more annoying, once everyone arrives for the annual Christmas house party, she can't stop watching Giles, and thinking about Giles. And kissing Giles, whether there's mistletoe about or not. Now Paul wants to marry her, and Giles wants to seduce her–and Serena has a bone to pick with the old wives who came up with all this superstitious nonsense in the first place.

PRAISE FOR ANNA CAMPBELL

"The Seduction of Lord Stone is romantic, emotional, sexy and funny. In fact, everything I have come to expect from Anna Campbell. I'm looking forward to reading the other Dashing Widows' stories." —*RakesandRascals.com*

"With her marvelous combination of humor and poignancy Anna Campbell writes in such a way that every story of hers has a special meaning and remains like a sentimental keepsake with those fortunate enough to read her work!" —*JeneratedReviews.com*

"Lord Garson's Bride is a well written and passionate story that touched my heart and sent my emotions on a rollercoaster ride. I particularly recommend this book for fans of convenient marriages, and those who enjoy seeing a deserving character find out that love is lovelier the second time around." —*Roses Are Blue Reviews*

"Campbell immediately hooks readers, then deftly reels them in with a spellbinding love story fueled by an addictive mixture of sharp wit, lush sensuality, and a wealth of well-delineated characters."—*Booklist, starred review, on A Scoundrel by Moonlight*

"With its superbly nuanced characters, impeccably crafted historical setting, and graceful writing shot through with scintillating wit, Campbell's latest lusciously sensual, flawlessly written historical Regency ... will have romance readers sighing happily with satisfaction."—*Booklist, Starred Review, on What a Duke Dares*

"Campbell makes the Regency period pop in the appealing third Sons of Sin novel. Romantic fireworks, the constraints of custom, and witty banter are combined in this sweet and successful story."—*Publishers Weekly on What a Duke Dares*

"Campbell is exceptionally talented, especially with plots that challenge the reader, and emotions and characters that are complex and memorable."—*Sarah Wendell, Smart Bitches Trashy Books, on A Rake's Midnight Kiss*

"A lovely, lovely book that will touch your heart and remind you why you read romance."—*Liz Carlyle, New York Times bestselling author on What a Duke Dares*

"Campbell holds readers captive with her highly intense, emotional, sizzling and dark romances. She instinctually knows how to play on her readers' fantasies to create a romantic, deep-sigh tale."—*RT Book Reviews, Top Pick, on Captive of Sin*

"Don't miss this novel - it speaks to the wild drama of the heart, creating a love story that really does transcend class."—*Eloisa James, New York Times bestselling author, on Tempt the Devil*

"*Seven Nights in A Rogue's Bed* is a lush, sensuous treat. I was enthralled from the first page to the last and still wanted more."—*Laura Lee Guhrke, New York Times bestselling author*

"No one does lovely, dark romance or lovely, dark heroes like Anna Campbell. I love her books."—*Sarah MacLean, New York Times bestselling author*

"It isn't just the sensuality she weaves into her story that makes Campbell a fan favorite, it's also her strong, three-dimensional characters, sharp dialogue and deft plotting. Campbell intuitively knows how to balance the key elements of the genre and give readers an irresistible, memorable read."—*RT Book Reviews, Top Pick, on Midnight's Wild Passion*

"Anna Campbell is an amazing, daring new voice in romance."—*Lorraine Heath, New York Times bestselling author*

"Ms. Campbell's gorgeous writing a true thing of beauty..."—*Joyfully Reviewed*

"She's the mistress of dark, sexy and brooding and takes us into the dens of iniquity with humor and class."—**_Bookseller-Publisher Australia_**

"Anna Campbell is a master at drawing a reader in from the very first page and keeping them captivated the whole book through. Ms. Campbell's books are all on my keeper shelf and _Midnight's Wild Passion_ will join them proudly. _Midnight's Wild Passion_ is a smoothly sensual delight that was a joy to read and I cannot wait to revisit Antonia and Nicholas's romance again."—**_Joyfully Reviewed_**

"Ms. Campbell gives us...the steamy sex scenes, a heroine whose backbone is pure steel and a stupendous tale of lust and love and you too cannot help but fall in love with this tantalizing novel."—**_Coffee Time Romance_**

"Anna Campbell offers us again, a lush, intimate, seductive read. I am in awe of the way she keeps the focus tight on the hero and heroine, almost achingly so. Nothing else really exists in this world, but the two main characters. Intimate, sensual story with a hero that will take your breath away."—**_Historical Romance Books & More_**

ALSO BY ANNA CAMPBELL

Claiming the Courtesan

Untouched

Tempt the Devil

Captive of Sin

My Reckless Surrender

Midnight's Wild Passion

The Sons of Sin series:

Seven Nights in a Rogue's Bed

Days of Rakes and Roses

A Rake's Midnight Kiss

What a Duke Dares

A Scoundrel by Moonlight

Three Proposals and a Scandal

The Dashing Widows:

The Seduction of Lord Stone

Tempting Mr. Townsend

Winning Lord West

Pursuing Lord Pascal

Charming Sir Charles

Catching Captain Nash

Lord Garson's Bride

The Lairds Most Likely:

The Laird's Willful Lass

The Laird's Christmas Kiss

The Highlander's Lost Lady

The Highlander's Defiant Captive

The Highlander's Christmas Quest

Christmas Stories:

The Winter Wife

Her Christmas Earl

A Pirate for Christmas

Mistletoe and the Major

A Match Made in Mistletoe

The Christmas Stranger

Other Books:

These Haunted Hearts

Stranded with the Scottish Earl

MISTLETOE AND THE MAJOR

CHAPTER ONE

Otway, Shropshire, Christmas Eve, 1815

Edmund Sherritt, Major Lord Canforth, pulled his tired horse up on the brow of the hill. Below him, the fine Jacobean manor of Otway Hall nestled in its pretty valley near the Welsh border. Early winter twilight descended, lengthening the shadows and turning the leafless trees to silhouettes against the darkening sky.

At last he was home.

Four days ago, he'd finally received permission to turn his back on a distinguished military career and return to civilian life. He'd left London at a gallop, traveling on horseback because he couldn't bear to wait for his carriage to be packed and ready.

North and west he'd ridden, eager and happy. The first night on the road, he'd snatched a few hours' sleep in a rough inn and set out at first light.

But as the miles from London mounted and the miles to Otway dwindled, he found himself unaccountably slowing down, taking his time. Lingering over meals. Staying in bed longer in the morning—he couldn't call it sleeping without making himself a liar.

One might almost imagine the gallant major delayed his arrival at the home he'd longed to see for close to eight years. If such an idea weren't inconceivable in connection with a decorated war hero, one might even wonder if the gallant major dallied because he was…afraid.

Of course that was absurd. Lord Canforth had served his country since the British army joined the Peninsular War in 1808. He'd been wounded at Waterloo, and once recovered, he'd spent the last few months crossing the Continent, working to establish the peace. Such a man would hardly quail at the idea of returning to his estates.

Afraid or not, he'd dawdled on the road, when by rights, he should already be sleeping in his own bed.

Even a sluggard's journey eventually came to an end. Now he paused above the landscape he loved more than any other. Whatever uncertainty he harbored about his reception, he felt long-delayed pleasure seep into his bones.

In any season, this was a fine view. Winter lay

lightly on the valley, creating a symphony of subtle greens and grays and browns. His gaze drifted across the gardens surrounding the house, and the bare woodlands rising behind it. The low hills encircled what to him had always seemed an earthly paradise. Brimming with happy boyhood memories of loving parents, and freedom and adventure.

Smoke curled from the house's chimneys. This close to Christmas, he hadn't been sure if anyone would be home to greet him. The coward who had possessed his soul since he'd returned to England last week had hoped the house might be empty, giving him a chance to settle in before he needed to worry about anyone else.

Of course he'd have to deal with people again. He was the Earl of Canforth, and he had obligations to his estate. But a few days alone would offer a welcome respite.

A few days before he had to meet the wife he'd married nearly eight years ago and hadn't seen since.

Felicity, Lady Canforth, emerged from the dark warmth of the stables, blinking against the gray light and carrying an empty bucket she intended to fill at the pump. The promise of snow edged the air. It looked like a cold Christmas ahead.

When the raw-boned bay horse clattered into the

stable yard, she didn't recognize it. Or the man bundled in hat, scarf, and greatcoat in the saddle.

This isolated valley didn't get many unexpected visitors. And it was odd for someone to come to the stables instead of the front door.

She straightened, annoyed at the intrusion, not least because in her brown pinafore, she wasn't dressed to receive guests. "Can I help you?"

The rider drew to a stop, and she felt him studying her from under the brim of the hat he'd pulled down low over his face. A thick green muffler concealed his features.

"I hope so," he said through the scarf.

"An introduction might be a nice start," she said pleasantly.

One gloved hand rose to pull away the scarf. "Don't you remember me, Flick?"

Dear God in heaven. Shock shuddered through her like a blow. Her legs threatened to collapse under her. The bucket crashed to the cobblestones where it rolled disregarded.

"Canforth?" The word emerged as a whisper.

Under her wide-eyed gaze, he unwound the scarf and, with a slowness that struck her as significant, he lifted away his hat. "The same," he said in a dry tone.

She barely heard through the blood rushing in her ears. Her heart raced like a wild horse as her hungry eyes devoured the man she'd last seen over seven years ago. Powerful joy and equally powerful uncertainty churned in her stomach, turned her knees to jelly.

She drank in every detail of his appearance. Over the years, his image had faded in her mind, despite her best efforts to cling to every memory. Thick auburn hair sprang back from his high forehead. The bony nose and jaw were the same. But there were other, obvious changes. Deep lines now ran between nose and mouth. His gray eyes no longer hinted at a continual smile. Most shocking of all was the long, angry scar that extended from temple to jaw.

That must have hurt like the very devil. At the thought of his suffering, she couldn't control a murmur of distress.

Her involuntary reaction made his lips tighten. He raised one gloved hand toward the saber slash—for surely nothing else could cause such damage—before he sat upright in the saddle and surveyed her down his long nose. "Or perhaps not quite the same, after all."

The pride was familiar. And the courage. He'd loathe her pity. She forced herself to pretend that she didn't want to drag him off that big, ill-tempered looking nag, and take him in her arms, and weep all over him like a fountain.

"Why didn't you tell me you were coming?" Keeping her voice steady required every ounce of willpower.

"I decided I'd beat any letter home." The deep rumble of his voice was the same, too. She remembered how it had always vibrated pleasantly in her bones. In the cold air, their breath formed clouds in front of their faces when they spoke. "On Wednesday, I got back to London from The Hague and found the orders that released me at last."

Felicity bent to retrieve the bucket, so that he wouldn't see the tears rushing to her eyes. She and Canforth had always been friends, but friends who made no undue demands on one another. Definitely not the kind of friends who howled and cheered and created a fuss when the wanderer returned from dangerous foreign exploits. She'd gathered from the first that he shied away from any hint of sentiment.

For a second, she fumbled blindly, until she found the handle. She rose with what she prayed was a fair appearance of composure. "The last letter I had from you was written in Vienna."

Through all these endless, lonely years, the only real reminder that she was a wife and not a maiden lady had been his letters. Written regularly. Delivered erratically, according to the rigors of war and travel. She'd written to him, too. He read her letters, she knew—he responded to her questions about managing the estate —but she had no idea what, if anything, they'd meant to him. For her, his every word had been air to a woman dying of suffocation. Although true to the unspoken contract between them, in her replies, she'd never ventured beyond news of everyday events.

"Good God, I must have written that two months ago. There's more to come."

"I look forward to them," she said easily, as if those letters hadn't kept her heart alive since he'd gone away. She set the bucket down near the pump.

"I always looked forward to yours." It sounded like mere politeness. But then he'd always been polite. Even during their few encounters in the countess's big oak bed, he'd treated her like a fine lady. Never like a lover.

"Let me hold your horse while you get down," she said, pushing away that unwelcome recollection.

Her husband was home and safe. For now, that was more than enough. Their difficulties could wait. After all, they'd waited nearly eight years already. Another few days wouldn't make much difference.

"You shouldn't be performing these menial tasks." He frowned. "Where in Hades are the grooms I pay a fortune to maintain?"

"I've given them a few days off for Christmas." When she caught the bridle, the horse eyed her balefully. "Most of the staff are on holiday."

"Do you mean you're here alone? At Christmas?" The frown intensified. "Why the deuce didn't you go to your parents? Otway's a hellish isolated place to spend the festive season. Especially if you've been mutton-headed enough to send the servants off."

"You know, a man who's been away so long should wait to see the lie of the land before he starts throwing his weight around," she said coolly.

When she'd married Canforth at eighteen, his slightest displeasure had terrified her. To her surprise, despite her piercing gratitude that he was back, she found it easy to stand up to him now. Seven years running the estate had lent her a measure of confidence sadly lacking in her younger self.

Her defiance elicited a grunt of sardonic laughter. "Perhaps he should. Forgive me. It's a damned long ride from London. I apologize for being a grumpy bear."

This willingness to admit he was in the wrong was familiar—and endearing. Her years in charge of Otway had taught her what a rare and precious quality that was in the male animal. Her tone became more conciliatory. "Actually I'm not altogether alone. Biddy's here. So is Joe."

"Are they?" Unalloyed pleasure filled his expression. An unalloyed pleasure absent when he greeted his wife. Ridiculous to be jealous of a couple in their sixties, but she was.

He slung one leg over the saddle and dismounted. To her horror, when he met the ground he staggered and almost lost his balance. The horse snorted and shifted under the clumsy movement.

"Canforth!" she cried, releasing the bridle and rushing forward to slide her shoulder under his arm. "Are you hurt?"

One gloved hand gripped the stirrup as he fought to stay upright. "Hell," he muttered. "I'm sorry, Flick. All day in the saddle."

"Can you walk?" she asked, as his weight pressed down on her.

She hadn't been this close to a man since he'd gone away. Yet the scents of healthy male sweat, horses and leather were heady and familiar. And his nearness reminded her how fragile and female she always felt when big, brawny Edmund Sherritt held her close.

"Yes, of course," he said, already transferring the burden from her.

"You never told me you were wounded." Although the hiatus in his letters about six months ago should have alerted her. Only the pallor under his tan betrayed what it cost him to stand on his own feet.

"A souvenir of Waterloo. Nothing serious."

Felicity believed that like she believed in fairies. She slipped her arm around his waist.

"Is the scar on your cheek from Waterloo, too?"

She needed all her courage to ask the question. That single betraying gesture when she'd first seen his face told her that he was self-conscious about his changed appearance.

Gently he disengaged himself. "My unearthly luck finally ran out under a French hussar's saber."

He'd gone through the entire Peninsular campaign with barely a scratch. Or at least so he'd told her. "After today, I'm not sure I trust you. Did you really escape injury so long?"

"Mostly."

Before she could sift that for its full meaning, he took a shuffling step forward and his left leg buckled.

Men and their pride! "Don't be a fool, Canforth. Let me help you."

The lordly displeasure returned to his manner, but he was sensible enough to accept her assistance, if with reluctance. He even deigned to place an arm around her shoulders, the heavy greatcoat scratchy against her neck. "This isn't how I wanted to come back to you."

"You've come back. That's all that matters." At a crawling pace, they made their way toward the house. "How many days have you been riding?"

"Four. This is the worst my blasted leg has been in months. I managed all that cavorting around the courts of Europe without too much trouble. I hoped my wound was all but healed—I had plans to dance with my pretty wife at the New Year assembly in Shrewsbury."

"Maybe the one after this." Braced under his weight, she angled toward the kitchen. He wouldn't have to deal with many steps, and there was a fire. She suspected the cold weather was responsible for at least some of his pain.

"What about my horse?" he asked, glancing back.

"Is he likely to bolt?"

"No."

"Then he can wait until I get his master inside, and I send Joe out to look after him. You need to get inside to warmth and shelter, not go chasing after horses that if they wander, won't wander far." She sent him a darkling look, expecting masculine outrage at the way she took charge. "And if you argue with me, I'll kick you in your sore leg."

She needed a moment to recognize the bass rumble as laughter. "Well, I'll be damned. You've changed, haven't you? I left behind a sweet little poppet, and I've come home to a managing virago."

"Get used to it," she said, even as she hid a wince. While he was away, she'd grown up a lot. She'd had to. But would he like the woman she'd become in his absence?

Now that the immediate shock of his arrival ebbed, she had a chance to regret how untidy she looked. She'd been seeing to the few horses left in the stables, and the navy blue dress under her pinafore was old and crumpled. She'd plaited her thick brown hair this morning, and it hung in a long braid down her back. She felt more like a milkmaid than the lady of the manor.

"Can you manage this step?" she asked.

"Yes," he said, and with some help from her, he did. Once they entered the short, icy cold passage that led to the kitchens, he drew away and supported himself with his hands on each wall.

Her heart ached to see his struggles, although she gave him his way. Stupid of her to miss him needing her. But he'd never needed her before, and she'd rather liked the experience.

Ahead, the thick door was shut to keep in the warmth on this freezing day. Felicity stepped forward and pulled it open to reveal a vast room lit by high windows.

Canforth loomed behind as she paused on the threshold. In front of the fire, a large, brindle hound staggered arthritically to his feet, turning his head this way and that. When his rheumy eyes settled on Canforth, he set up a long, keening howl. He limped toward the door, rushing so fast on his rickety legs that he almost fell in a tangle with every step.

"Digby?" Canforth said, and Felicity heard the awed disbelief in his voice. "Digby, old boy."

The tears that had threatened since Canforth's return stung her eyes, and she swallowed to shift the boulder of emotion in her throat. On unsteady legs, she stepped aside as Canforth stumbled forward into the room to greet the dog.

For the first time, she read raw emotion on his face. The pain and loneliness of his years of exile lay so stark on her husband's features, that she had to turn away to save her heart from breaking. She dug her fingernails deep into her palms to control her tears.

When she had herself under control, she watched the reunion. Dog and master, equally clumsy in their urgency, met in the middle of the kitchen. Digby's howl rose to a crescendo that bounced off the stone walls. His old tail wagged so hard that his bony haunches bumped from side to side.

Canforth had forgotten his wound, but Felicity hadn't. When he stripped off his gloves and dropped to his knees, she rushed forward to catch his elbow and help him down to the floor.

"Digby. Digby, old lad." He kept muttering a litany of loving nonsense to the dog. Catching Digby's head between his hands, he rubbed the floppy ears. The dog's howl subsided to high-pitched whimpers of frantic joy.

When Felicity stepped back, she raised her hands to her cheeks and found they were wet. This emotional meeting tore her composure to shreds. She envied Digby's freedom to give vent to his happiness, whereas she had to pretend that Canforth's return wasn't a wonder to end all wonders.

She retreated against the stone wall and flattened her palms behind her to keep from interfering. Not to hug man or dog. Not to protest at the pain the man visibly suffered as he kneeled to pet and praise the dog with broken, half-coherent pleasure.

At last, Digby's burst of energy faded, and his canine excitement ebbed to a low, continuous whine. Felicity wiped her eyes and sucked in a shaky breath.

By the time Canforth looked up at her, she'd regained a little poise. His vulnerability lingered. The sardonic fellow from outside had disappeared. She hoped for good.

"I was sure he'd died. He must be close to fifteen."

She swallowed but still had to speak past a lump in her throat. "I'd have told you if he'd gone."

He patted the dog, who gazed up at him in an

ecstasy of adoration. "You mightn't have known how much I love him."

Love... Such a potent word, and one she'd never heard her husband use before.

"Of course I know." Her voice remained husky, but she couldn't do anything about that. "During our fortnight together, he was your shadow."

"He's well?"

She managed an unsteady smile. "Right now, he's ready to fly to the moon."

This time when Canforth's gray eyes settled on her, they were warm. "Thank you for looking after him for me."

"Oh, Canforth," she said helplessly, wanting to cry again. "Don't be such a fool. I tried to look after everything for you. I just pray I succeeded."

He stared into her eyes, and she saw deeper into his soul than ever before, even the few times when they'd shared a bed. Especially the few times they'd shared a bed. "Thank you for that, too."

She blinked back more tears, and when he spoke, she had a feeling that he tried to save her from succumbing to unseemly emotion. Unseemly emotion had never been part of their marriage. "He must be deaf as a post."

She gave a laugh, cracked but genuine. "He is, at that. And close to blind."

"He won't like that at all. How he used to love chasing rabbits." With an open affection that made her heart ache anew, he ran his hand over the dog's graying head.

"The rabbits of Otway Hall thrive untroubled, as you'll see."

Digby butted his master's thigh to regain his attention, and Canforth smiled down at him with transparent fondness. "It's all right, old chap. I'm here now, and I've got no plans to go away again."

The smile made him look younger, more like the man she'd married than the stern stranger who had ridden in today. It also made the abomination of his scar stand out harsher than ever.

The Earl of Canforth had never been conventionally handsome, but his features had been remarkably appealing, conveying intelligence and interest and kindness. The scar seemed incongruous, cruel. But then, Felicity had always thought the man she'd married, with his gentleness and whimsical humor, wasn't born to be a soldier. Yet he'd fought valiantly through years of arduous campaigning. He'd been mentioned in dispatches, promoted, and decorated, and she'd heard—not from Canforth—that Wellington had called him one of the bravest men he knew.

Her husband was a complex creature. Even as an inexperienced girl, Felicity had known that. The question was what state was he in, now he was home. And what were his plans for life after the army? For himself, the estate. And his wife.

Could she and Lord Canforth establish a life

together after so long apart? She'd been so young and naïve when they'd married, and they'd only had two short weeks together before he embarked for Portugal with his regiment. In most ways, they were strangers yoked together for life.

She reminded herself to let this day be sufficient unto itself. There was plenty of time to sort out the future. Every decision needn't be made the instant her husband arrived home.

"Your leg must be hurting. And it can't be good to rest your knee on those hard flagstones." She stepped forward and spoke calmly, now she'd regained some vestige of control. "Let me help you up."

Felicity waited for his pride to reject her offer, but he let her assist him with reasonably good grace. She knew despite his discomfort, he did his best to keep his weight off her. Digby didn't make it easy either, winding about his master's legs and threatening to trip him.

She gripped Canforth's hand to keep him from falling and frowned down at the shiny skin that covered his fingers. More scars. These looked like burns. The pain must have been unimaginable. She bit her lip against more tears. With every moment, it became clearer that he'd been through a hell even worse than the one she'd pictured. And he'd never thought to confide in his wife about any part of it.

"Young Master Edmund!"

The quavering voice took Felicity by surprise and

made her look toward the entrance to the pantry. Digby's whimpering had masked any sounds of approach.

Canforth turned so fast, he almost overbalanced. "Biddy!"

"Oh, Master Edmund." The old woman burst into noisy tears and flung herself at the earl. "Your poor, poor face. What have those wicked Frenchies done to you?"

"It's all right, Biddy." He patted her shoulder and returned her embrace. "It's all right."

"But look at you," she sobbed. "I can't bear it."

"I was never very pretty, so no great harm has been done."

"What nonsense is that?" The old lady wrenched away and placed her hands on either side of his head so she could inspect him. "I always thought you were a handsome lad. And my lady agrees with me."

Canforth gave his old nurse a lopsided smile. "My lady was just being polite. She didn't marry me for my looks."

"Of course she did. And your good, kind heart. She was smart enough to love you."

Felicity was blushing like a tomato. "Biddy, give the poor man a chance to take a breath. He's only just walked through the door."

"And needs feeding up, I'll warrant." With visible reluctance, she released Canforth and mopped at her streaming eyes with her apron. "Don't mind me. I'm just a foolish old woman. But it's a red letter day indeed when the master comes home at last. A red letter day."

He smiled at her. More of that easy kindness that Felicity had first noticed when she'd met him in a London ballroom eight years ago. She'd feared this sweetness might be an early casualty of the violence on the Continent. But miraculously, she already saw that it remained essential to the man she'd married.

"You're not foolish at all, Biddy." He laid a scarred hand on her shoulder. Both hands were burned, Felicity noticed with a pang. "And I've missed you like the devil."

Biddy smiled through her gushing tears. "Oh, get away with you. I'm sure as sure you hardly gave me a thought while you were off teaching Boney a lesson. But heaven has answered all my prayers when I see you home now."

"Back to stay, I hope."

"I'm glad you've had enough of strange foreign parts. The Earl of Canforth belongs at Otway."

"Indeed he does," he said.

"Now get away out of my kitchen. This is no fit place for your lordship. Or your ladyship, come to that. Although I have to say there's no airs about your countess, Master Edmund. You brought home a treasure there. While you've been away, she's run this estate almost as well as you would. A fine wife you caught for yourself." She made shooing motions. "But listen to me, rattling on. When you two haven't seen each other in a donkey's age. Go on upstairs and find out all that's happened while you've been apart. And I'll make a veal and ham pie for supper. That was always your favorite."

Canforth leaned in and kissed Biddy on the cheek. Felicity couldn't help but compare the affection flowing between him and the old servant with his constraint toward his wife. After the long separation, some awkwardness was inevitable. But in this case, the awkwardness between the earl and his countess dated back to their wedding.

"If you knew how often I dreamed of your cooking when I made do with stale bread and salt beef, on some freezing peak high in the Pyrenees."

"Not right, just not right." The old lady clicked her tongue in disapproval. "And look at you now, you're too skinny. I swear you're like a piece of string, you're so thin. Leave it to me, and I'll get some meat on your bones. You haven't been looking after yourself. Anybody with eyes in their head can see that."

He laughed. "I'll be as fat as a prize pig by spring, Biddy. I promise you."

A confident step on the staircase down from the great hall heralded the arrival of Joe, Biddy's husband, stout and gray-headed and taciturn. At the sight of the new arrival, a rare smile creased his lined face. "Your lordship, by God, you're home. This is a great day indeed."

The old man, less demonstrative than his wife, embraced Canforth, but Felicity caught the shine of tears in his eyes as he drew away.

"Joe, will you please look after his lordship's horse?" she said. "It's out in the stable yard, if it hasn't bolted."

Joe bowed to her. "Aye, my lady. Although begging your pardon, but there's no fear of that happening. No horse ever bolted that Edmund Sherritt rode. Putty in his hands, they are. Always have been."

Once, women had been putty in his hands, too. Before his marriage, Canforth had had a reputation with the ladies. Felicity had been surprised that he'd been so diffident when he'd come to her bed. Since then, she'd struggled to avoid the thought of him being anything but diffident in some pretty senorita's company.

So many years away, and a man was sure to get lonely. After all, it wasn't as if he loved his wife back in England.

Since he'd left her, she'd slept alone. But then, she loved her husband and always had.

CHAPTER TWO

Felicity was pleased to see Canforth moving more easily, now he was out of the cold. Her silly, worried self wanted to fuss and question, help him with the stairs. But she made herself precede him slowly up to the great hall, so he wouldn't be too self-conscious about his limping progress.

Digby struggled after them even more slowly. It was clear he had no intention of parting from his master. Doggy panting accompanied them all the way. Felicity couldn't help contrasting the easy conversation downstairs with the silence that now descended.

"Shall we go into the drawing room? Joe lights a fire in there each evening."

When Canforth didn't answer, she glanced back. He leaned on the doorway cut through the carved screen, and if she didn't know better, she'd imagine him unchanged from the man she'd married. The gathering dusk hid that vicious scar, and his casual posture belied the way he favored his leg.

His expression wasn't casual at all. Avidly his eyes took in every detail of this vast room, the heart of the medieval building around which the rest of the manor had grown. She read such a range of powerful reactions in his face. Love. Sadness. Joy. Relief. Curiosity.

"It's just the same," he said in disbelief.

"Of course it is." Poignant emotion threatened to choke her once more. She'd better gain control of herself soon, or abandon any pretense that she and Canforth shared a dispassionate marriage.

"It's mad, I know." He paused, and she knew he battled for composure. "But through all the bloodshed and destruction, I'd think back to this house as a site of perfect happiness, until I was convinced it couldn't possibly be as I recalled it."

His intense tone made Digby whine and bump his grizzled head against his master's hip. Canforth laid one elegant, scarred hand on the dog's neck and looked around. "You've even put up the kissing bough. Did you guess that I was coming home?"

Stupidly Felicity blushed. During her honeymoon, kisses had been infrequent. In fact, she and Canforth hadn't acted much like a honeymoon couple at all. He'd treated her with respect and kindness. And she, so young and inexperienced, hadn't known how to ask for more. Especially once she reached the conclusion that Canforth had no argument with a temperate marriage.

"I held a party for the staff before I sent them off to their families for Christmas."

He cocked an eyebrow at her. "So did you kiss a handsome footman or two?"

She affected an airy tone. "Oh, these days, the grooms are prettier than the footmen."

He laughed and stepped fully into the room, Digby at his side. "You're warning me about the competition?" He stopped under the colorful ball suspended from the ceiling. "Shall we, wife?"

Puzzled she looked at him. "Shall we what?"

He pointed up at the woven ribbons and mistletoe and holly. "After nearly eight years, a kiss doesn't seem too much to ask."

Heavens, she hadn't blushed this much since she was a new bride. "You want to kiss me?" she asked shakily.

He rolled his eyes. "Flick, you're my wife, and it's been a long, cold road since last I saw your pretty face. For charity's sake, give me a kiss. On my honor, I'll make sure it doesn't hurt."

That was the second time he'd called her pretty. Despite telling herself it meant nothing, warmth flooded her veins. "I'm sadly out of practice."

"I should hope so." He stretched out his hand. "But I think we'll manage the basics."

With hesitant steps, she approached Canforth and took his hand. The shock of contact zapped through her like lightning.

"You're trembling," he murmured in surprise, as he drew her closer.

"I told you it's been a long time."

He positioned her under the mistletoe bough and placed his hands on her slender shoulders. "There's no need to be frightened."

Except it wasn't exactly fear she felt. Felicity was nervous and keyed up, but not scared. She avoided his eyes, not wanting him to see her tumultuous reaction.

Logic had told her that the end of hostilities in Europe meant her husband's return. But as the months went by, with Canforth posted from one capital to another, she'd started to think he might stay in the army. True to the impersonal tenor of their letters, he'd never mentioned his long-term plans.

When nothing happened, Felicity made herself look at him. The sight of that vile sword cut made her want to scream and rage.

He winced under her stare. "The surgeon who sewed it up said it will fade with time. Give me another twenty years or so, and I'll be back to the dashing devil you married."

Self-disgust ripped through her. He made a joke of it, but she saw that he'd interpreted her anger and compassion as revulsion. "Oh, Canforth, you mistake me," she cried, daring to move closer. "I hate to think of you being in pain."

The flash of uncertainty in those deep-set gray eyes

told her that he didn't quite believe her. "I got out pretty lightly."

"But I can't bear it when someone I…" *Love.* "…care for suffers." Her hand hovered over the raised flesh. "Does it hurt to touch?"

He watched her with a strange fascination. "No. Not now."

She bit her lip, hoping she wasn't breaking the unspoken truce they'd always operated under. But she couldn't let him think she found his appearance repulsive. "Will you trust me?"

"Only if you can bear it."

She saw the bone-deep weariness beneath his happiness to be home. The years had been hard for her. How much harder must they have been for him, far from everything he loved? She didn't count herself in that list. Love had never been part of their marriage, even if she'd loved him from the first moment she saw him, tall and commanding in his scarlet uniform, across a crowded ballroom.

"Oh, Canforth," she said, her heart breaking anew. Gently, she laid the tip of her index finger at the top of the scar.

At the contact, he recoiled, then stood still and tense beneath the mistletoe. She blinked away more tears and slowly traced the slashing arc. For some reason, she expected the scar to be cold, but the puckered, shiny skin was warm. Just as much part of him as the rest of his face.

He closed his eyes, thick russet lashes fluttering on his prominent cheekbones. She'd always loved this hint of softness in such an overtly masculine being. Under her fingers, he remained as taut as a violin string. How could a man who had withstood cannon fire fear a woman's touch?

"If he'd cut an inch higher…" she whispered.

"I was lucky."

"So was I."

His eyes flashed open, the enlarged pupils turning the gray irises smoky. "Do you mean that?"

"Of course I do." She frowned in bewilderment as she lifted her hand away. "How could you think otherwise?"

Her brain advised resisting the impulse, but her heart made her lean in and place a fleeting kiss where the saber had sliced deepest. The clean outdoors scent of his skin invaded her senses and made her heart skip a beat.

"I haven't been much of a husband," he muttered, as she drew away.

"You did your duty to your king and your country." She swallowed to shift the painful emotion jammed in her chest. "You've made me proud."

"Really?"

"Really." Her voice was husky. "You're a brave man, Lord Canforth. And if you don't think I'm overjoyed that you've come back safe…"

"If a trifle battered."

"If a trifle battered." She managed a twisted smile. "Then that saber cut has affected your mind."

She was close enough to hear his long exhalation of relief. "I wasn't sure how you'd feel."

"That's natural." Fighting the urge to fling her arms around him and tell him that she loved him, she stepped back. She'd already ventured too close to revealing her feelings. Such a kind man would hate to know that she suffered, loving him when he didn't love her. And her pride revolted at the idea of his pity. In that, they were alike. "After so long apart, we need to rebuild our friendship. You've only been home an hour."

His lips quirked. "At least give me until dinnertime to feel like I'm back to stay."

She made herself smile again, although she remained closer to weeping than laughter. "Before you know it, you'll be ordering me around and demanding your claret and tobacco and slippers like a real lord of the manor."

"First, we have unfinished business here under the mistletoe. I've waited a devil of a long time to kiss my wife."

The sudden purpose in his expression sent sensual awareness rippling along her spine. Her lips burned from the brief kiss, however chaste, she'd given him. She was blushing again.

Blast this odd situation. She was both wife of eight

years and bride of a couple of weeks. There was no solid ground beneath her feet.

When gentle fingers tilted her chin up, she caught her breath. He brushed his lips across hers in a kiss that was over almost before it began. She'd braced for something more passionate, which was absurd when he'd never shown her anything but the most delicate handling. The few times he'd used her body, he'd treated her as if the slightest roughness would damage her.

It hadn't been enough then. It certainly wouldn't be enough now. She was eight years older than that naïve girl. After Canforth left, she'd learned the meaning of longing.

The kiss was like a whisper. But even such brief contact turned her knees to water. Instinctively she reached toward him, to bring him closer.

Before she could touch him, he stepped away, leaving her floundering. "That was a fine welcome," he murmured and gave her a brief bow, as if they'd only just met.

She remained poised under the mistletoe, lips tingling, although it was clear there would be no more kisses. "I'm so glad you're home, Canforth."

Her sincerity seemed to surprise him. He subjected her to a searching inspection, before giving her the rare, sweet smile that always turned her blood to honey.

"I'm glad, too." Then just as powerful currents

threatened to crack the veneer of politeness, he looked around. "Will you excuse me? I'm covered in travel dirt, and I'd like to change into some clean clothes before dinner."

The shift to practicality jarred after that vibrant instant, when she felt they'd hovered on the brink of some profound revelation. "Everything is just as you left it when you went away. Is there luggage coming?"

"I left a few things in London. I'm sure I can make do with whatever's here."

Over the years, Felicity had learned to put away deep and painful emotion and play the efficient chatelaine. "I'll have hot water sent up. Do you mind if dinner is early?"

"Not at all. I'm famished. Shall I see you in the drawing room in an hour?"

"That will be lovely."

She needed to go downstairs and make arrangements for the evening with Biddy and Joe. A different man and a different woman might rush from greeting to bed. Passion long denied would find quick and furious release.

But she and Canforth had never been wild for one another. More was the pity. Since he left, her bed had been a cold and lonely place. Apparently after doing his duty with no particular urgency on their honeymoon, he'd returned from the wars no hungrier for her body. Her husband was back, and she felt lonelier than ever.

Felicity watched Canforth limp toward the stairs—

standing so long under the mistletoe hadn't been good for his leg—and told herself she had so much to be grateful for. The husband she loved was home and safe. He seemed pleased to see her. He remained the kind, considerate man she remembered.

A little too considerate, she thought, before she told herself to behave.

Anything more was a romantic dream that she must relinquish if she hoped to find a scrap of happiness in this marriage.

But as he turned out of sight around the bend of the staircase, she glanced up at that absurd kissing bough with its promise of easy, light-hearted pleasure. Disappointment settled heavy and sour in her stomach.

CHAPTER THREE

*C*anforth felt as nervous as a cadet on his first parade, instead of like a seasoned soldier of thirty-two, when he fronted at the drawing room on Christmas Eve.

His exquisite wife always made him feel like a bull at a tea party. She was so slight and graceful and perfect. The first time he saw her, he'd known Flick was the one for him. But he'd never quite conquered his shyness in her company. It was ridiculous, when he was capable of playing the rake with any other woman.

But then no other woman had ever mattered.

When they met, Flick had been sweetly innocent and unsure of herself. He'd wooed her gently, and that gentleness had continued into their honeymoon. They'd never quite fallen into being at ease with one other. Perhaps with more time, they'd have found their way. But he'd received his orders a fortnight after the wedding, and he'd had to leave her, still closer to a stranger than a wife.

That constraint remained as a gulf between them. She'd been shaking like a leaf when he kissed her under the mistletoe. While he'd been away, her image had fueled a thousand fantasies. But faced with the real Flick, any hope of a passionate reunion evaporated.

Ah, well, he was home now, and this time he'd do his damnedest to build a real marriage.

He'd feared that she'd find him repulsive, scarred and injured as he was. But there had been no mistaking the care in her touch when she'd traced his scar.

His Flick had a gallant heart. He'd never doubted that. The doubt was whether she'd grant that heart to him, the way that he'd granted her his at their first meeting.

When he came through the door, Digby at his heels, his wife sat sewing by the fire. Gratitude soothed the strife in his soul. Over the years, he'd dreamed about more than bed sport. He'd also longed for sweet domesticity. The comforts of home. A woman's gentle voice to greet him. The promise of quiet happiness, stretching ahead like a golden road.

He sucked in a breath of air that didn't stink of unwashed humanity, gunpowder, and blood. And felt his heart settle into a steady rhythm of hope.

He loved Flick. In time, she might come to love him. Once she'd recovered from her surprise, she'd been glad to see him. He'd wager eight years of a major's salary on that. And after conquering her bashfulness, she'd accepted his kiss.

It wasn't enough. But it was a start.

Canforth smiled as he watched her over her embroidery. She attacked the stitching with the fierce concentration she devoted to everything that caught her attention. He recalled her searching stare the night they met, as if she already knew their first dance would change their lives forever.

This evening, she wore an elegant pink gown. What a contrast to the charming ragamuffin he'd discovered when he arrived. Now her shining mahogany hair was arranged in a loose knot that set off the pure oval of her face. He had a sudden fantasy of seeing her hair cascading around her shoulders when he came to her bed. Sexual hunger thundered through him and shattered the peaceful mood. When they'd married, he'd wanted her like the very devil. Controlling his lustful urges had been a constant battle. All these years without her had only fed his endless craving.

Something of his agitation disturbed the air, and she looked up, her sewing falling disregarded into her lap. Her coffee-colored eyes widened, and for one sizzling moment, he wondered if she longed, too.

Then she put aside her embroidery hoop and stood up and smiled as she would at a casual acquaintance, and he knew wishful thinking had caught him out again.

"Canforth, let me get you some wine."

He walked into the room, trying not to limp. He loathed returning to her in such a mess. "Thank you."

She stepped across to the decanters, arrayed on a Sheraton table. He observed her confident air with interest. The self-assurance was new. His shy bride had been so unsure of everything. But of course, she'd been chatelaine here the whole time he'd been away, and done an excellent job running the estate and his other business interests.

"Or would you rather have brandy?"

"Claret is fine." He subsided into the seat opposite hers. An involuntary groan of pleasure escaped him as his weary body sank into the cushions. He'd spent a deuce of a long time on horseback this last week. Digby pressed heavily against Canforth's thigh, fortunately the good one. His hand dropped to fondle the dog's ears. "Come in to sit by the fire, have you, you pudding-headed mutt?"

A low laugh escaped Flick as she poured the wine. "He's made do with me all these years. But I always knew I was second best."

Canforth stared hard at the woman he'd married. She'd been an enchanting girl, but this more mature version fascinated him. "You're second best in nothing."

He'd loved how his new bride had blushed, although her modesty left him feeling perpetually guilty about his lascivious thoughts. He was pleased that he could still make her go pink. And over the years, the lascivious thoughts had only intensified.

"Thank you. Is it good to get off your leg?"

"After four days in the saddle, I'm looking forward to staying in one place." He accepted the glass she passed him. Digby settled down, propping his nose on Canforth's ankle. "But most of all, it's good to be home."

She returned to her seat, and the glass of wine she'd poured before he appeared. "You're looking better already."

He rubbed one hand over his now smooth chin. He'd arrived looking like a vagabond. A wash and a shave, and changing out of his uniform made him feel like a new man.

Or more likely, the sight of his lovely wife made the difference. Which reminded him…

"We'll have to visit London, or at a pinch Shrewsbury once Christmas is over. None of my clothes damn well fit anymore."

"You've grown sadly thin on army rations." The hint of fondness in her smile made his foolish heart leap. "Perhaps Biddy and I should just do our best to feed you up in the next week or so."

"I've returned to you much reduced. I suffered a fever after Waterloo. It left me close to a skeleton."

Distress darkened her coffee-colored eyes, and he cursed himself for mentioning his wound. Especially on this first night, when he edged toward establishing a rapport with his wife. He was surprised and delighted that she didn't feel nearly as much a stranger as he'd expected.

"You never told me. Even after you recovered and started your secret missions to secure the peace."

"I didn't want to worry you."

She frowned. "Yet you must have known I'd worry anyway."

"Did you? I'm sorry. I always tried my best to protect you from the worst of what happened."

"I know, and I appreciate your consideration." Irony twisted her lips. "But even someone as sheltered as I've been understood that fighting the French across Spain and Portugal was more than a carefree picnic in the hills."

He took a mouthful of wine, savoring the excellent vintage. He'd shoot himself before he drank another drop of sour Spanish red. "When we wrote, we didn't venture beyond trivialities. You didn't give me any bad news from here either."

"You didn't need the added burden of hearing about troubles at home—especially when we always managed."

"You never spoke of your feelings. I found myself wondering whether you were happy or sad, lonely or fulfilled, busy or bored."

Her expression turned somber. Once more, he noted how the girl he'd married had changed into a strong and intriguing woman. "Right from the start, we never spoke about our feelings. And you never asked. I assumed you preferred to keep our communication on a superficial level."

"And in turn, I assumed that's what you preferred," he said softly. "We knew each other so little when I left to join my regiment."

"Now we've been blessed with a second chance," she said, equally softly. Unspoken lay the words, "when so many others didn't survive to pick up the threads of family life." She sent him a straight look. "Let's not waste it, Canforth."

"No, let's not."

Flick's wry smile shifted the heavy silence. "My tales of the household and snippets of village gossip must have struck you as frightfully flimsy."

With a grunt of amusement, he bent to rub his wounded thigh. His leg felt better with every hour he spent away from his horse, but it still ached. "I won't countenance anyone speaking ill of those letters. They saved my life."

Doubt and gratification vied in her expression. "You exaggerate."

"Perhaps a little. But not if I say sanity rather than life. So many times, you gave me a smile when things were at their grimmest. And your letters reminded me what I was fighting for."

She mightn't have discussed her feelings or her worries in the letters that arrived so faithfully over their long separation. But that didn't mean they'd revealed nothing about his bride. Her courage and steadfastness in his cause had been impressive, if no surprise. But what a beguiling discovery her quirky humor had been.

She blinked, and he caught the shimmer of tears in her pretty eyes. Then to his regret, she looked toward the fire, although her voice trembled with feeling. "That's a beautiful thing to say. I'm sure those silly letters are unworthy of such praise."

"There was general rejoicing in the camp when mail from Otway arrived. We eased many an icy night in the Pyrenees with news of Miss Kelso's pursuit of the vicar, or the antics of Mr. Brown's delinquent pig."

She took a sip of her wine. "Miss Kelso caught Mr. Harvey in the end, you know."

"We toasted her success with the worst rotgut swill I've ever had the misfortune to swallow."

Flick's eyes held a trace of her early shyness as she glanced back at him. "It's true that you read those frivolous stories out to a hardened band of soldiers?"

Canforth raised his hand as if taking an oath. "On my honor. Never underestimate the power of a bit of whimsy and a few jokes to cast light into impenetrable darkness. You were a heroine to my entire troop, Flick."

Her eyes glowed with pleasure. "Oh, I'm glad. When I started to write, I had no idea what might interest you. I'm afraid I was much less generous with your letters. I hoarded them all to myself."

His letters had been shorter and considerably less

prolific. But every time he wrote, he felt like he made a promise to himself that one day, he'd return to the woman and the life he loved. "I like that."

"Now I'm really pleased I didn't pour my girlish heart out to you."

He shrugged. "I'd have liked that, too."

"No, you wouldn't," she said in a dry tone. "And your men certainly wouldn't have."

With a brief laugh, he relaxed back in his chair and let the half-empty glass dangle from his fingers. "Perhaps not."

He'd soon learned to read between the lines in her letters. Lack of discussion of feelings didn't mean a lack of feelings altogether. For either of them.

Before he'd left her, he'd never found the right time to speak his love. Whenever he set out to tell her, uncertainty about her feelings put a padlock on his tongue. The act of sitting down to write, even in the midst of ruin and chaos, had been a way of offering his wife his deepest devotion. And while Flick's letters might not have declared her love, they proved that she thought of him and cared enough to write.

"Canforth, I know your life has been grueling and dangerous, and there are things you will never wish to speak about. Or at least not on the night you return home." She paused, her grip on her wineglass tightening. "But some day, when you feel at ease, and you're truly back in the world you left behind so long ago, will you tell me?"

He flinched, before he realized how his reaction betrayed the numberless horrors he'd witnessed. "Flick, it's not pretty."

Her lips tightened, but her brown gaze remained steady. "Nevertheless I want to know."

As he stared at her, his instinctive objections faded. The girl he'd married couldn't have coped, couldn't even have comprehended. But the woman of twenty-six who had fought her own battles, she perhaps might understand.

"In that case, then, yes. One day. One day when I'm ready, I'll tell you a little of what it was like."

"Thank you." Her lips turned down in a self-derisive smile. "And I owe you an apology. That was a poor welcome I gave you. An empty house, and a wife stinking of the stables."

Actually when he'd first touched her, he'd caught the scent of crushed flowers and something that was Flick alone. He'd remembered that fragrance immedi-ately—it would always be the aroma of heaven. There might have been a hint of horse and hay, too, but he hadn't cared. He'd been too busy fighting the urge to bury his face in her hair and tell her how much he'd missed her. Which would have ruined things between them forever. If he leaped on her like a starving wolf the minute he came home, she'd run for the hills.

"It's still my home, empty or not, and I gave you no warning I was coming. But you haven't told me why you're spending Christmas alone."

She took another sip of wine. "I didn't feel like going through all the hullabaloo this year. It...it seemed easier to miss you here at Otway than in a noisy, happy crowd of people, however much I love them."

Shock made him sit up straight and stare at her. "You missed me?"

The question surprised her. "Of course."

"But I've been away for ages."

She gave a grim laugh. "I know."

By Jove, that was dashed nice to hear. Dashed nice. To think, she'd missed him. Perhaps his case wasn't quite as hopeless as he thought. He leaned back and stretched his legs toward the fire, making Digby grumble at the interruption to his snooze. "Well."

A smile lit her eyes to burned caramel. "Well, indeed."

She set aside her wine and picked up her sewing, as if she hadn't changed his world in the space of a second. "It means a plain Christmas dinner, I'm afraid. A returning hero deserves to have all the stops pulled out."

Another silence fell, this one more comfortable than the last. Canforth finished his wine and let its warmth fortify the warmth seeping into his blood with every moment in his wife's presence. For years, he'd been cold and lonely. Was his exile finally at an end?

He'd had no idea what welcome awaited him at Otway Hall. But this hadn't been it.

Although so far, he had no complaints. He and Flick

had never managed a proper conversation before. He prayed this was only the first of many to come.

"Compared to some of the places I've been since I left you, this is luxury indeed," he said, as if there had been no break in the conversation. She'd been brave enough to admit she'd missed him. He could be brave, too. "And having you to myself for a few days without worrying about an army of servants or an influx of guests is perfect."

She looked up quickly. "Really?"

"Really."

She drank from her wineglass to hide another blush. And he still found it charming. "Would you like to go to the midnight service?"

He shook his head. "I'd rather keep my head down for a couple of days, before the villagers discover I'm back. Is that too ungodly?"

"No, it makes perfect sense. If you'd come back to a house full of servants, keeping your arrival quiet would be impossible. But Biddy and Joe won't gossip, and this gives you a chance to settle in without anyone bothering you."

Not quite true. His wife bothered him a great deal. "Will you go?"

"Oh, yes. I have so many reasons to be thankful."

She smiled, and his lingering misgivings about the future faded to a distant rumble. He was home. He had time to make everything the way he wanted it.

"So have I. But I'll say my prayers in private. I doubt the Lord will mind."

Biddy bustled in. "Dinner's ready, and I hope you both enjoy it, as it's a night for celebration. This Christmas Eve is full of miracles, when we've got the master home at last. Her ladyship has had a dire lonely time of it since you went away, my lord."

He caught another faint blush on his wife's cheeks, but to his surprise, Flick didn't deny it. "It is wonderful, isn't it, Biddy? We don't need any other Christmas present. Nothing could be as good as knowing my lord is safe and well, and back where he belongs."

Moved, Canforth stood, stumbling as he put his weight on his injured leg. He appreciated his wife's tact in not offering to help, although he knew she watched over him with care. By nature, he was independent, but he was infernally pleased that Flick concerned herself with his welfare.

He extended his arm as Digby struggled to his feet with not much more grace than his master. "Shall we go through to dinner, my lady?"

CHAPTER FOUR

hen Felicity returned from the midnight service in Otway's small stone church, her heart still brimmed with gratitude. Joe and Biddy had accompanied her, and if only the three of them knew the special cause for rejoicing this Christmas, that was good in the Lord's eyes, she was sure.

Now she stood in the countess's bedroom, separated from the earl's bedroom by a narrow dressing room, and tried not to resent sleeping alone yet again. She'd slept alone for the vast majority of her marriage. What was one more night?

Except she was agonizingly conscious that if she walked through the dressing room, she'd find her husband asleep in his bed. As she'd returned through the freezing night, she'd wondered whether Canforth would wait up for her. The thought had made her tremble with wanton anticipation.

But she'd arrived back at the manor to a note wishing her a good night and a merry Christmas, and saying he'd see her at breakfast. However foolish it might be, she'd kissed the slashing signature, familiar after his hundreds of letters. Thank goodness nobody saw her doing such a nonsensical thing, or she'd have been mortified.

She'd seen enough of the world now to recognize that Lord Canforth had been a remarkably circumspect bridegroom. During their honeymoon, he'd come to her bed a mere five times. She'd been shy and woefully unprepared. The only child of elderly parents, the marital act had proven a complete shock. Despite her husband's patience and tenderness, she'd cried and cowered away on their wedding night.

On the few occasions he'd returned to her, he always treated her with heartbreaking consideration. Gradually she'd started to find pleasure in what he did, but he left before she felt at ease in a man's embrace. Even a man she loved.

He'd abandoned her to yearn, but with no memory of satisfaction to comfort her. She'd spent the years since, wishing she'd been braver, more responsive, more welcoming. She hadn't been a cold bride, but nor had she been a particularly generous one. Constant regret had eaten at her. Regret, and the gnawing fear that she'd never have the chance to be a real wife to Canforth.

Fate had granted her a second chance. She meant to seize it.

Bold words. When her husband slept in his room, and she hovered, uncertain and awake, in hers.

Perhaps he no longer wanted her. Perhaps he'd never wanted her, and that tentative honeymoon was proof.

Except he'd wanted her enough to propose. And he'd written to her all these years. Tonight when she'd looked into his eyes, she'd felt a new and powerful connection linking them.

Surely that couldn't be just on her side.

After that conversation in the drawing room when they'd ventured closer to confidences than ever before, they'd retreated to lighter subjects over dinner. Canforth had been exhausted, and while he did his best to hide his discomfort, she knew that his leg wound troubled him. She'd bitten back the urge to chide him for not taking a carriage, instead of riding all that way in the cold.

Tomorrow was Christmas. Today, really, although it wasn't long past midnight. A decent sleep might restore him. Perhaps tonight, he'd come to her bed.

If only she could enlist the mistletoe's magic to make her marriage what she wished. Canforth mightn't love her, but she wanted him to know that while he'd left a frightened girl behind, he returned to a woman eager to be his wife in every sense.

Feeling more optimistic, Felicity changed into her white flannel nightgown, plaited her long hair, and picked up her book. She prayed that next time she lay down, she had something more exciting than "The Vicar of Wakefield" to put her to sleep.

Around her, the old house settled into silence.

The first groan was quiet. Some animal in the woods outside could have made the sound.

The second, hard upon the first, was louder and unmistakably human.

Felicity set down her book and swung her feet to the floor. Should she go to Canforth? Or would he consider it an unforgivable breach of his privacy? He'd always come to her bed, with no traffic in the other direction at all.

Curse this strange half-marriage.

Another long cry, sharp with misery, swept hesitation aside. One would need a heart of stone to disregard the anguish in the sound.

Springing to her feet, she grabbed her candle and burst through the doors separating her from Canforth. When she raised her candle to reveal the large man writhing on the bed, she saw he was too lost in the throes of his nightmare to notice any noise she made.

She paused on the threshold, tossed back to the uncertain girl she'd been, in awe of her big, strong husband. After a fraction of a second, the capable chatelaine took over. Digby raised his head from near the fire, but seeing Felicity, he lay down again, as if he knew his master was in safe hands.

She hoped to heaven he was right.

Despite the cold night, Canforth had kicked the blankets to the floor. The sheet twisted around him. In the flickering light, a sheen of sweat covered his bare chest and shoulders.

"Canforth." With surprising steadiness, she set the candle on the nightstand and leaned over to place a soothing hand on his shoulder. "Canforth, wake up. You're having a bad dream."

He didn't wake, but he turned violently in her direction, like a compass needle pointing to north. The lines of suffering on his face made his scar stand out like a red banner.

Pity so powerful that it hurt gripped her. She'd known he must have seen and done terrible things, but only now, witnessing this unconscious torment, did the truth stab deep into her soul.

"Canforth, wake up," she said in a firmer voice.

This time he jerked away, dislodging the sheet completely.

She gasped, although the bare torso should have warned her what to expect. He slept naked. Ridiculous after eight years of marriage to discover that.

Even as her hand began to stroke him into calmness, her hungry gaze devoured the magnificent sight before her. Like so much else during their time together, he'd been reticent about his nakedness, coming to her in a dressing gown and taking her in darkness. He hadn't even removed her nightdress.

As his ragged panting eased, she surveyed this man she'd married.

Biddy was right. He was too thin. Felicity knew that, even before he'd appeared at dinner in clothes that had fitted eight years ago and now draped loose on his rangy frame. But his thinness made the superb lines of his body stand out in stark relief. The broad shoulders and powerful chest. The ribs clearly delineated under the pale skin. The narrow hips and long legs. She winced to see the knotted scar on his thigh. He'd called himself lucky, and in many ways he had been. But he'd bear his scars until the day he died.

Inevitably her gaze strayed between his legs, where his rod lay soft in its nest of dark auburn hair. She bit back the forbidden impulse to touch it, even as her fingers curled at her side.

Without looking away, however brazen that made her, Felicity bunched her bare toes against the cold wooden floor to restore some circulation. She hadn't waited to put on a robe and slippers before she dashed to Canforth's side. The night was freezing, despite the fire burning in the grate.

When she looked up, her husband's eyes were open. She blushed like fire and whipped her hand away from his shoulder.

"Flick, you're here?" he said hoarsely, grabbing her hand hard enough to bruise.

"Yes," she whispered. Meeting that glassy stare, she realized that the dream still gripped him.

Instinctively, although physical contact between them had always been rare, she smoothed the damp strands of hair back from his high forehead. Beneath her touch, his skin was clammy. At least the dream hadn't heralded a return of his fever.

"It's all right. There's nothing to worry about. Go back to sleep." How incongruous to speak to this huge, virile man the way she would to a child. But for all his potency and power, she was achingly aware of his vulnerability at this moment.

She'd bitterly regretted that their short honeymoon hadn't resulted in a child for her to cherish during his long absence. Warmth flooded her, when she realized that now Canforth was home, children might lie in their future. How wonderful that would be.

"Flick, you're here," he said again, although she remained unsure that he was awake. At least the horrors receded from his gray eyes, and his deathly grip on her hand loosened.

"Yes, I'm here," she said, still combing her fingers through his hair with a languorous pleasure that felt wicked. She'd itched to touch him like this since he'd returned.

His hold tightened. "Stay with me."

Her heart somersaulted with a giddy mixture of

excitement and nerves, as she stared into eyes clouded with sleep and the ghost of his dreams. She tugged her hand free and bent to straighten the bed, pulling up the blankets. With a deep sigh, he rolled onto his back and closed his eyes.

After stoking the fire, she blew out the candle and slid in beside him. Unsure how to proceed, she, too, lay on her back, clinging to the edge of the mattress and shivering with cold.

Canforth had dropped back to sleep. He lay mere inches away, breathing deeply and steadily. Whatever cruel memories had disturbed his slumber, they seemed to have receded now.

She'd felt so bold joining him. Now her courage deserted her. A braver woman might cuddle into his side or wake him with kisses. Felicity remained where she was, her heart racing. Surely she wouldn't sleep a wink.

This dream had tormented Canforth a thousand times before. He woke in a soft, warm bed that smelled of Otway, a million miles from the rough, cold ground of the Pyrenees. It was dark, but dawn wasn't far off. His wife slept, trusting and relaxed, in his arms. He was naked, and hard and ready for her. The sweet scents of home and Flick tinged the air. He was safe, and free to linger as long as he wanted in bed with the woman he loved.

He lay on his side, his chest pressed to Flick's back. She was tucked against him in perfect peace, her head resting on his outstretched arm. His other arm curved around her, one hand cupping her breast.

For a delicious interval, he basked in this imaginary paradise. Soon enough, there would be orders and maneuvers, and later, the likelihood of violent, bloody mayhem. But right now, he could give himself up to the fantasy that he was back at Otway, and all was well with the world.

As nobody yet seemed to be clamoring for his presence, he let the dream spin toward its end. Usually some interfering blockhead dragged him back to brutal reality before he got too far.

Drowsily he bumped his hips against the perfect curve of Flick's rump. He buried his nose in the fragrant mass of her hair and breathed in her rich scent.

Today's dream was particularly vivid. Most times, Flick was naked, but on this occasion, his imagination taunted him with a flannel nightgown between him and her skin. The breast in his hand had the weight and feel of reality, and when his thumb flicked her nipple, it hardened with gratifying swiftness. She made a sleepy sound of encouragement and nestled closer.

Dreading the inevitable awakening, he shifted and rolled her toward him. He reached down to lift the plain nightdress—next time he had this dream, he'd dress her in silk. Or nothing at all.

She made another of those damned suggestive murmurs and arched against him. He slid his hand between her legs, seeking her hot, silky core. She wriggled in welcome, and he kissed her neck until she quivered with eagerness. He didn't dare open his eyes. Not now. Not when, even if only in his mind, rapture hovered so close.

His lips drifted lazily over her face until they met hers. So soft. So full. The kiss's sultry sweetness shuddered through him.

"Canforth," she breathed in ardent invitation.

Odd. In his fantasies, she always called him Edmund.

He stroked her cleft until she was slippery and ready, and slid one finger inside her, to find the slick honey of her arousal. As sleek heat coated his finger, he leaned in and kissed his wife with a carnal hunger he'd always leashed when he'd had her, virginal and fragile, as his bride.

Dream Flick responded as she always did.

Well, not quite. She opened her mouth and put her arms around him to bring him closer. But her endearingly clumsy kisses were an enchanting reminder of the girl he'd left so long ago.

Canforth rose and positioned himself between her thighs, desperate to claim her. By God, this was the best dream he'd ever had. If his tomfool sergeant interrupted him now, he'd shove the fellow in front of the nearest firing squad.

In wordless welcome, she tilted toward him. He groaned into the warm curve of her neck, the scent of her sleep-warmed skin the sweetest fragrance in the world. He bit down on the sensitive nerve and heard her gasp with rising excitement.

He lifted his head and opened his eyes.

Damn it.

Astonishment gripped him, banished disappointment. Instead of a rough tent pitched on an Iberian mountainside, he saw a familiar bedroom, shadowy with a dying fire. And the woman beneath him was no figment of his imagination, but his beautiful, fastidious wife.

"For pity's sake, Flick, why didn't you stop me?" So close to possession, it was sheer agony to pull back. But he managed it, over the howling, excruciating protest of every muscle in his body.

She bit lips swollen and red with his kisses and stared up at him. "I..."

Before she could go on to call him a beast and a brute, and every other name he deserved, he rushed into speech. "What the deuce are you doing here?"

She flinched at his belligerent tone and wrenched her hands from around his neck. He rose on his arms above her and struggled to settle down. But with her lying so close, it was impossible. His restraint balanced on a knife edge.

"You had a nightmare," she stammered. "You were calling out."

"Hell, I'm sorry."

Vaguely he remembered the old horrors visiting him last night. He hadn't had that dream in months. Returning home had stirred up too many strong emotions. Returning home, and seeing Flick.

Canforth always woke from his nightmares, sweating and gasping and unable to go back to sleep. Flick's presence must have calmed him, allowing other, much more appealing dreams to take over.

She looked hurt. "You don't have to apologize."

"Yes, I do. I hoped to give you time to get used to me again, before I resumed my husbandly rights."

The light wasn't bright enough for him to see her blush, but he was sure she did. He waited for her to express relief, but she stared up at him as if nothing made sense. Then her delicate jaw firmed. "We've already waited more than seven years, Canforth."

"Believe me, I've counted every day." It was his turn to demur. "But I'm not sure I can be careful with you tonight, Flick. It's been too long."

Unambiguous annoyance crossed her face. "I don't want you to be careful. I'm your wife, not a Meissen shepherdess you keep on the mantelpiece."

"But what I just did—"

"Was wonderful. For once, I thought that you really wanted me."

He gave a snort of disbelief. "Want you? I die of desire for you."

Her eyes widened. "You do?"

"Yes. And I can't bear to think I might hurt you because I've lost control of myself."

"I'm not made of glass, Canforth." This time her frown was thoughtful, rather than displeased. "And anyway, I want you, too."

"You do?" He remembered those unpracticed but enthusiastic kisses. They hadn't been the product of his imagination. They'd come from a woman discovering sexual pleasure and frantic to experience more of it.

"You do," he said more slowly.

Tentatively she hooked her hands over his shoulders. Even such a light touch shuddered through him like an earthquake.

Flick's voice emerged as a strangled whisper. "I've been lonely for so long, Canforth. I don't want to be lonely anymore."

CHAPTER FIVE

*I*n an agony of suspense, Felicity waited to hear Canforth's response to her plea. Had she pushed too far? Broken their unspoken truce? Proven she was no lady, but a brazen trollop?

But he said he wanted her. And even in her inexperience, she'd recognized his hunger when he'd turned to her in his dream. And there was no mistaking the hot male weight pressing against her stomach. Whatever his mind or his conscience might say, his body showed unequivocal interest in taking things further.

When he started to pull away, her heart plummeted into her stomach. Failure tasted rank on her tongue.

God forgive her, she'd made a mistake. Been too forward, too needy, too…real.

"I'm sorry," she muttered, lifting her hands from his shoulders.

"What are you sorry for?" he asked, rolling off her

and sitting up. The fire didn't provide much light, but she made out the powerful outline of his chest and shoulders against the shadows. Even too thin, he remained an impressive figure of a man.

"For…for asking…" Her voice faded to nothing, as she sat up and faced him.

"Silly goose." White teeth flashed as he smiled. "You have nothing to apologize for. Believe me."

He caught her hand and carried it to his lips. The kiss he brushed across her knuckles made her tremble —and hope.

"Canforth?" she asked uncertainly.

He kept hold of her hand, and his eyes glittered as they focused on her. "After all this time, do you think you could bear to call me Edmund?"

Ridiculous to balk at such an intimacy when not long ago, his finger had penetrated her body with astonishing and arousing effect. The memory of those sizzling caresses still heated her blood. "Are you sure?"

"Only if you feel comfortable. But you're my wife. I'd feel privileged if you used my Christian name."

She nodded. "In that case, I feel privileged, too, Edmund."

Those straight shoulders eased, and he released a long breath. She couldn't imagine why he cared what she called him, but it was apparent that he did. "You do an old military man's heart good."

"You're not old," she said quickly. "You're in the prime of life."

"I've come back to you a physical wreck."

Despite the darkness, her hand unerringly found the scar on his cheek. With an aching tenderness that she hoped he felt, she traced the line of the cut. "I told you—as long as you've come back to me, I don't care."

"Ah, Flick," he said, her name a soft exhalation. "You never told me why your parents called you Flick."

"When I was a toddler, I couldn't pronounce Felicity. Flick was as close as I got."

"Would you rather I called you Felicity?"

She shook her head. Did he know he continued to hold her hand? It was odd—nice—sitting in the darkness on Christmas morning and swapping confidences. "No. I…like the way you say Flick."

"I like that I have a special name for you."

"So do I." Her fingers tightened on his, and she said a silent prayer for him to stay. Now and forever.

But it seemed heaven wasn't listening, because he released her and rose from the bed.

Despite her resolution to be brave and make no demands, when he was so newly returned home, a hum of distress escaped her.

"What is it?" Edmund turned and studied her through the winter gloom.

She wanted to lie, but the unadorned truth emerged. "Don't go."

His laugh was a rumbling undertone. "My dear wife, wild horses wouldn't drag me away."

"Then what are you doing?"

He shifted toward the fire, presenting a breath-taking view of his naked back and buttocks. Despite favoring his left leg, he moved more freely than he had yesterday. He'd blamed last night's pain on the long ride in the cold. She hadn't been sure whether to believe him, or whether he tried to protect her from learning the full extent of his injuries.

"Because I want to do this right." Edmund stoked the glowing embers in the hearth, then gave Digby a pat and a murmured word, before placing a couple of logs on the fire.

The revitalized flames illuminated his noble profile, with its high forehead and arrogant nose and defined jaw. He looked at ease in a way she'd never seen. As if he'd worn a mask of politeness and carefully main-tained consideration, but now the mask fell away to reveal the real man.

Silently, Felicity watched the everyday movements, while her heart crashed into an excited gallop. Beyond those unsatisfying encounters in her bed, they'd never enjoyed the quiet intimacy of sharing a room. Tonight a fragile thread twined them together. She felt married to this man she loved in a way she never had before.

The air quivered with the promise of pleasure. A rich tide of anticipation washed through her, and she stretched against the rumpled sheets like a cat in the sunlight. She'd never felt like this. So full of love that she was likely to explode into a volley of stars.

Edmund lit a couple of candles and placed them

on the mantel, setting the room aglow. He turned to face her as she pushed upright against the pillows. A man's body remained in many ways a mystery, although she gloried in the changes from the sleeping Edmund to this awake, fully aroused version.

Her fingers clenched in the sheets. She itched to touch him, to explore those hard planes of muscle and bone so different from her soft curves.

"Shall I fetch my robe?"

The old, shy Felicity would have hidden her head under the covers by now. Tonight she took her time assessing this man she'd married so long ago. "No."

A faint, pleased smile curved his mouth as he returned to lighting candles.

The frankness of her desire surprised her. She'd always loved Edmund, but never before had her love felt so earthy. A hot weight settled in the base of her belly, craving for his skin against hers, the heated meeting of bodies.

He paused in his preparations, and their eyes conducted a simmering but silent conversation. Invitation and acceptance. She wanted what was to come more than she wanted to take her next breath. Pray God she wasn't mistaken, but what she saw in his face told her that he felt the same.

"Take down your hair," he said quietly.

With unsteady hands, she loosened her plait until her hair cloaked her shoulders. Edmund gave another of those heavy exhalations, as if he'd been holding his breath for hours.

"This is what I dreamed about." He stepped forward and gripped the carved base of the bed. The candlelight shone on the cruel burns across the back of his hands. "Now take off your nightdress."

Felicity swallowed to moisten a dry mouth, even as she moved to obey. With a bit of maneuvering, she tugged the thick flannel nightdress over her head.

She was blushing. Of course she was. But her eyes were steady as they met his. She rested against the piled pillows and let her hands fall open at her sides.

"You're so beautiful," he murmured. "You beggar my fantasies."

"I'm glad."

"You'll think me a satyr, but so often in the hell of the Peninsula, I pictured you just like this. Army life provides no sweetness, just incessant brute masculinity. But in the few quiet moments, I'd close my eyes and think of the woman waiting for me at home."

"I don't think you're a satyr at all." Her heart cramped with love, and stabbing compassion for all he'd sacrificed in the name of duty. "I wish I'd known you thought of me. It would have been a comfort."

"Of course I thought of you. Constantly." His eyes sharpened. "Did you think of me?"

She didn't try to hide her surprise and pleasure at his confession. "All the time."

"And did you wait?"

She took a second to understand what he asked; it was so far from the reality of her solitary life these last years. "I've had no man but you in my bed, Edmund." She paused before admitting the dangerous, awkward truth. "I've wanted no man but you in my bed."

Triumph turned his gray eyes silver. "I hoped. I guessed."

He was glad. That must mean something.

Felicity linked her hands over her bare stomach in an attempt to calm her nerves. She was painfully conscious of her nakedness. How she wished he'd touch her, so she didn't feel quite so on display. But this might be her only chance to ask the question that had troubled her since he left.

Her voice emerged as a husky murmur. "I know I really have no right to ask this. The world views a man's needs as so much more urgent than a woman's, after all. And it's so many years. And you made no promises of fidelity before you went away…"

Edmund's expression was unreadable. "Yes, I did. When we stood before the altar, I vowed to be faithful."

She frowned, trying to make sense of what he said. She couldn't have heard him right. If she had, surely it must be too good to be true. "You mean—"

His gaze remained unwavering. "I mean I've had no woman in my bed since I left your side."

She struggled to contain her relief and happiness. Her husband wasn't a liar. She knew that. But still his claim pushed the limits of belief. "That must have been difficult."

A sardonic grunt of laughter escaped. "Not that difficult. I married you because you're the only woman I want. I don't need a substitute."

Wide-eyed, she stared at him. However unlikely his story, she found she believed him. Even the part about him wanting her. Every word he spoke radiated sincerity.

Joy surged, strong enough to wash away old doubts. "I had no idea."

One hand made a sweeping gesture. "Why the devil else did you imagine I proposed?"

She shook her head. "I thought you needed a wife."

A faint snort. "So anyone would do, even you?"

"I come from a good family, and I brought a fat dowry."

He frowned. "You do know you're speaking arrant nonsense, don't you? You're the prettiest girl I've ever seen. I took one look at you across that ballroom, and I knew I'd met my destiny."

"Oh," she said breathlessly, desperate to keep her heart from taking wing and flying up into the heavens. None of this was exactly a declaration of love, but she now saw she'd badly miscalculated his emotional stake in this marriage. A trembling hand reached down for the sheet.

"Don't."

She met eyes ablaze with yearning. No matter how

awkward she felt, sitting here without a stitch to cover her, she couldn't deny him. She left the sheet where it was.

"So why did you marry me?" he asked.

Because I loved you so much, I felt likely to perish of it.

But although they'd done so much to bridge the distance between them, admitting her love remained a step too far. Traces of her old shyness lingered, for all that she sat naked before him.

"I liked you." That much she'd dare. "I still do."

He arched questioning auburn eyebrows. "That's a damned lukewarm reason for accepting a fellow."

Stupid to blush, when she'd made no secret that she wanted congress with her husband. "You were a catch."

He shook his head. "Not good enough. That season, you had a duke's heir and a marquess after you, not to mention a couple of baronets who could buy and sell me ten times over."

She ventured a little more honesty. "You were the only one who made my heart beat faster. And you were always so kind and gentle."

He looked horrified. "You make me sound like a dashed milksop."

She smiled. "No. There's strength in your sweetness. You're the bravest, best man I know. I was a naïve country girl when I accepted you, but I've never been sorry about my choice."

Edmund shifted as though her praise brought equal pleasure and embarrassment. "While you were smart and lovely, and I couldn't believe my luck when you said yes. I've never regretted my choice either, but you were so pure and untouched, I feared my passion would terrify you."

"I've always been stronger than you knew."

"I see that now. But you trembled in my arms and cried the first time I came to you. And you seemed no more reconciled to my attentions by the time I left."

"It was all so…overwhelming." She was old enough now to see how her reticence had hurt him, broken the trust between them. Blast her shyness and her ignorance. "And I wasn't sure what you wanted of me."

"You didn't like it?" he asked gently.

"At first, what you did was so outlandish, I was frightened. By the time you left, I'd started to enjoy our encounters." She looked down into her lap to avoid his eyes. "I liked that you made me feel I was the center of your world."

"You were." His jaw squared with determination. "You are. You must know that by now. I wonder that you were uncertain of it then."

Warmth flowed along her veins, feeding a frail optimism. He wouldn't say these breathtaking things if he didn't mean them. "You were always in such a hurry to leave afterward, I was sure I'd done something wrong."

"Never." Guilt darkened his expression. "But what I wanted was so primitive, so all-encompassing, I held back for fear of giving you a disgust for the act. And for me. I couldn't trust myself not to turn to you again and again. Yet you felt so fragile in my arms, you deserved my care, not my fierceness."

Her smile contained a fair dose of remorse, too. "And because you showed me such care, I felt you didn't care."

His hand tightened on the base of the bed until the knuckles shone white. "Never think I don't care, Flick."

She gave a broken laugh. "Edmund, it seems we're both victims of our good intentions. If I'd known you wanted me, I'd have been braver. At least after the first time."

He still looked troubled. "We didn't know how to talk to one another then."

"But we know better now."

His expression was austere. "My prayer every night I was away was that I'd live to come back to you."

"And mine was that you'd live to come back to me."

"We've been fools."

She shifted against the sheets in a futile attempt to ease the insistent heat between her legs. "We have."

A sensual glint entered his eyes. "Do I still make your heart beat faster?"

She extended one hand toward him. To her surprise, it didn't tremble. But his admissions tonight had taught her a measure of courage. "Why don't you come closer and find out?"

To her regret, he didn't immediately take up the invitation. "If I touch you now, I won't be kind. I'll use you to the limit. I've starved for you, and only your complete surrender will satisfy me."

Ooh, that sounded so exciting. A wanton thrill rippled through her, and her toes curled against the sheets.

"Show me," she whispered. "Show me, before I die of wanting you."

CHAPTER SIX

When he stepped out from behind the base of the bed, Canforth felt the heat of his wife's gaze on his naked body. As she leaned amongst the pillows, admiration brightened her eyes, and something very much like desire. With a shock, he realized that a frailer version of that desire had always been present. Even from the first, when he'd been too blinded by her virginal delicacy to see.

He hoped to hell that his rapacious need didn't kill that precious longing. He'd tried to warn Flick what she invited. Once he was heaving about on top of her, she mightn't be so encouraging. But now that she was willing and within reach, he could no longer hold back. For God's sake, he was only human.

The sight of her threatened what little remained of his precarious control. His eyes devoured her from the top of her ruffled head to her slender bare feet. Damn it, but she was a glorious creature. Slim and graceful. Piquant face under a cascade of mahogany hair. Satiny, white breasts, crowned with beaded nipples, like rubies in the snow.

He stopped beside the bed and took her hand, his pulses jolting at even such an innocent contact. When he met her shining eyes and read the hunger there, he knew she was ready. He'd always felt like a hulking monster beside her, but tonight they'd unite as naturally as a wave ran up a beach. His attention lingered on the feathery curls at the apex of her thighs, and he thanked heaven for granting him this chance to discover her secrets.

What he'd learned already left him reeling with surprise. To think, she'd wanted him when they married. Even more wondrous, she wanted him now. And despite time and distance, they'd both stayed true to their marriage vows.

Flick raised her chin, and the steady courage in her eyes made his heart soar. "I'm not afraid, Edmund."

Never had he loved her more. His blood seething with impatience, he kneeled next to her and kissed her. Another of those ravenous, passionate kisses that had turned his dream to fire, before he'd discovered that it was no dream. Flick responded with more of that unpracticed fervor that risked burning him to a cinder. His injured leg protested all this movement, but he ignored it.

He slid his tongue into her mouth, savoring her rich

flavor. A sound of encouragement emerged from deep in her throat, and her hands crept around his neck, pulling the hair at his nape. The sting intensified the fierce sensations assailing him.

In a fever of need, he kissed Flick all over, tasting the silky skin at her collarbone and inside her elbows, and the delicate pattern of blue veins across her breasts. He nipped and sucked at her nipples, making her cry out and dig her nails into his shoulders. When she undulated against him in unabashed demand, he saw stars. He stroked between her legs, until she moaned and writhed. A gush of feminine arousal rewarded his caresses.

On a groan, he dragged her under him. Her brown eyes were open and glittering with excitement. He kissed her, torn to the point of torture between building her arousal and seeking his satisfaction. Knowing he had no choice, when he'd wanted her so long and so desperately.

With a sultry smile, she cupped her hand against his scarred cheek. "Don't wait another second, Edmund. Not one more second."

He sank into another kiss, succulent and hot. His hips jutted forward, and he slid into her body. Controlling the pace of his entry threatened to rip him into a million pieces. By heaven, she was tight. Through the furious blood pounding in his ears, he heard her murmur in discomfort. He paused and sucked in a jagged breath, battling for restraint. When he scraped his teeth along her neck, she shuddered, and her body softened, letting him edge deeper.

Canforth could hardly endure the pleasure streaking through him. Pleasure mixed with pounding frustration. He burned to plunge inside her, claim her to the core, find his consummation. Only possessing her would assuage the agonizing absence of the last years.

"Trust me, Flick," he muttered. "Let me in."

She made an incoherent murmur and tilted to meet him. He kissed her again, advancing into delicious resistance. Sucking in the warm, musky scent of her skin, he buried his head in the crook of her shoulder. Her breath was humid and erratic on his ear, and her arms clasped him closer.

For an excruciating moment, he lingered to let her adjust to his invasion, before even that delay asked too much. With a guttural groan, he seated himself fully within her.

She cried out and clenched hard around him. When he raised his head to look at her, her eyes were dark and heavy, and flags of color marked her delicate cheekbones.

He was a large man, and she was slightly built. When they'd first married, this discrepancy had troubled him, made him fear he'd hurt her if he yielded to his passions. Now it turned out that they were a perfect fit. Flick shifted with voluptuous languor, and

Canforth felt the change of angle like a blast of trumpets.

"Are you all right?" he murmured.

"I love having you so close to me. Don't stop."

He doubted if he could. Her throbbing heat turned the world to gold. This union was extraordinarily profound. He'd loved her from the first, but he'd never before felt that their souls meshed into one entity, while their bodies entwined in sensual bliss.

Resting deep inside her, basking in the snug welcome, the horrors of war faded to nothing. At last he was home. He released a shuddering breath and gave himself up to pure pleasure.

Canforth became preternaturally aware of a host of marvelous physical details. The radiant, sleek heat where they joined. The brush of her nipples against his skin. Her long hair tickling his scarred hands. The way her legs cradled him. The scent of arousal thickening the air.

Piercing joy filled him, but the transcendent stillness couldn't last. His body tightened with the need to move, to push forward, to seek the explosive ending to his endless longing. Every muscle tensed in anticipation. He kissed her hard. "Hold on."

Luxuriating in the barrage of wild sensations, he withdrew, then thrust to the limit.

Felicity jerked under the ruthless invasion, even while pleasure flooded through her. As Edmund drove into her like a conqueror, she sank under his weight and strength. His animal hunger was astonishing. She arched up and crossed her legs over his back, holding him close.

With startling speed, her incandescent delight in his passion spiraled beyond her control and became something greater. Something unfamiliar. Something focused not on his pleasure in her, but on her pleasure in him.

A ravenous hunger that wanted to swallow the universe in one bite coiled in her belly, tighter and tighter with every thrust of his body. She moaned and dug her fingernails into his shoulders, as the volley of sensations intensified. The flagrant carnality of this union left her shaking. She poised giddy on the edge of some terrifying, glorious, inescapable precipice. The breath crammed in her lungs, and she closed her eyes in excitement and fear.

Edmund growled as his movements became less controlled. He bucked against her, making the grand old bed creak. How she relished his uninhibited need. How she relished her untrammeled responses.

Yet still she teetered on the brink of the chasm, desperate to cross over, but unsure how to break across the final barrier to whatever waited on the other side. Tears of frustration clogged her gasping breath.

"Come over with me," Edmund whispered into the

side of her neck as he plunged, pushing her deep into the mattress.

This was like a war. But magnificent and untamed and brilliant, too.

"I can't…"

She strained against him, but that mysterious ending hovered beyond reach. Her blood thundered like a stormy sea, and her muscles ached with frantic longing. He pounded into her, his movements choppy and urgent.

"You can," he almost snarled. He tensed and thrust his hand between her legs to the source of that insistent ache. When he touched her hard, she bowed up and stepped off into clear air.

The old Felicity shattered into a million sparkling crystals. She cried out on a high, pure note and shuddered into a release so exquisite and overwhelming, it was like streaks of lightning ripped through her.

At last she was flying. As she soared, wild and free, she clung tight to the man she loved.

With another long groan, Edmund jerked in her arms. Through her quaking upheaval, she felt the hot spurt of his seed.

When at last she floated down from the outer reaches of bliss, she realized that her cheeks were wet. Edmund sprawled over her, crushing her into the bed. The scents of sex and satisfaction weighted the air.

Fighting dizziness, she gulped in a shallow breath to ease her burning lungs. Dear God, she'd have to tell him to move soon, or end up suffocating. But how could she bear to push him away? She'd never felt so close to him, even when he'd slid inside her, or when he'd yielded to shuddering release. Through the lonely years, this closeness was what she'd longed for most of all. After that rapturous flight that split the heavens wide open, she couldn't yet bring the connection to an end.

His big, strong body felt loose and exhausted in her arms. He breathed in great gusts, and his skin was damp with clean male sweat. She couldn't doubt that she'd satisfied him. As he'd satisfied her. When until tonight, she'd had no idea what satisfaction meant.

A wry smile curved her lips. How absurd to discover the joys of the marriage bed eight years after speaking her vows.

Felicity turned her head to kiss the cheek he pressed against hers. In this radiant aftermath, tenderness vied with sated desire. With a lazy caress, she ran her hand over his thick red hair, marveling at its silkiness. Her husband was such a fascinating mixture of the gentle and the strong.

Although it meant she could finally snatch a full breath, she was disappointed when he shifted. "Hell, Flick, I must be squashing you flat."

"I like it," she admitted softly.

"Thank you." He rose on his elbows and bent to kiss her with a piercing sweetness that melted her bones to syrup. "That was unforgettable."

She stared up into gray eyes, glowing in the candlelight. "Welcome home, Edmund."

He kissed her again with more of that soul-stirring care before he rolled to the side, separating their bodies. At the prospect of his departure, she couldn't contain a sound of distress.

From the day she'd agreed to marry him, she'd promised herself that she wouldn't ask for more than he was willing to give. But after what they'd just shared, everything had changed. She was about to break that particular promise.

"What is it, Flick?" He leaned over her, brushing her tangled hair back from her forehead. "Did I hurt you? All these years, the thought of you has driven me mad. I wasn't as considerate as I might have been, damn me for a careless brute."

She caught his hand and kissed it, feeling the hard, shiny skin of his burns under her lips. When had she and Edmund become so physically demonstrative with one another? On their honeymoon, they'd rarely ventured much past the marital act. Her fears had crippled her, inhibited her natural impulse toward showing affection.

Was it possible that her husband, for all his worldly experience, had felt a similar diffidence? Difficult to imagine dashing Edmund Sherritt as shy, but looking back with the advantage of maturity, she wondered if that might explain their mutual awkwardness.

"You're not a careless brute. And I love what we

did." She blushed, which was ludicrous, given her recent passionate responses. "I hope we'll soon do it again."

A smile curled his lips, and he kissed her. Who knew he was a man who liked to kiss? Certainly not the woman who had married him so many years ago.

"It's a safe wager that we will. I was in such a goddamned rush to have you, I missed a few things that require attention."

In this bed, he'd transported her to another world. She couldn't imagine feeling more wonderful than she had on that wild journey through the stars. Yet now it seemed she had more to discover. How thrilling.

"Oh?" Anticipation heated her blood. "Such as?"

He cupped her breast and brushed his thumb across the peak with an idle caress. "Every inch of your body deserves a week of admiration."

Her nipple beaded into a tingling point, and that swirling restlessness in her belly stirred anew. How on earth could she be interested in love play, when she'd only just found rapture beyond her wildest dreams? "A mere week?"

"On my first foray." Sitting up, he swung his legs over the side of the bed. He wasn't quick enough to hide a wince of discomfort.

"Edmund, I forgot about your leg." Felicity scrambled out of the bed and darted around to kneel in front of him.

"To be frank, so did I," he said roughly, rubbing the long scar.

"We should have been more careful." She brushed his hand aside to check if the wound had opened. When she saw no blood, she sighed with relief. "We could have done serious damage."

"Wanting you and not having you was more painful than anything the Frenchies could do to me."

Her unthinking dash from the bed proved that she had aches and pains of her own. She'd adored the headlong urgency of Edmund's passion. Now a few twinges reminded her that she was unaccustomed to having her body stretched and pounded.

When she studied Edmund, she didn't mind. He looked tired, but happy. And younger than the man who had ridden in yesterday afternoon. Her hand tightened on his thigh above his wound. "Please don't leave me."

"Leave you?" He frowned in puzzlement. "What rubbish is this? I've only just come home."

When she shook her head, her unbound hair slid against her newly sensitive skin. "Now." The word was a thread of sound. "Don't leave me now. I've wanted you for so long, I can't bear to be apart from you tonight."

Comprehension lit his eyes, and he stroked her hair, stretching his long legs out on either side of her. "I'm not going anywhere. And neither are you."

"Good." Giddy with relief, she kissed his thigh, just

below his stirring rod. A wicked thrill sizzled through her, gave her the nerve to place a kiss on the part of him that had offered her such superlative service. Her senses opened to a deep musky scent and the salty taste of his skin.

"Hell's bells," he gasped and plunged his hands into her untidy mass of hair, tipping her face up. "Where on earth did you learn to do that?"

Felicity flushed and regarded him uncertainly. "Didn't you like it?"

A strangled laugh escaped him. "I liked it beyond measure."

"It seemed a natural thing to do."

He bent down and this time, his kiss was urgent. "You, my wife, are a gift beyond price."

"When you kiss me like that, I can't think." Flustered, she pulled back and rose to her feet. With every movement, she felt the slickness between her thighs.

Edmund relaxed against the pillows and watched her with drowsy pleasure. "Come back to bed."

She sent him a quick smile. "Not yet."

When Felicity picked up her nightdress and hauled it over her head, he groaned and rolled his eyes. "You tease me."

She wandered into the dressing room. "Only a little."

"Flick, you'd better plan to come back here," he called with gratifying impatience.

As she opened the door to the huge rosewood

armoire in the corner, she smiled. How very nice it was to have a gorgeous man eager for one's company. "In a moment."

She returned, burdened with a large mahogany box. His face alight with curiosity, Edmund pushed up against the bedhead. "What the devil is this?"

Feeling very pleased with herself, she braced to extend the heavy box in his direction. "Happy Christmas, my dear husband."

He took it with a delighted smile. "I'd forgotten."

"So had I, even though I've just been to church."

He grinned and caught her hand for a quick kiss. "How clever of you to have a gift for me."

Felicity perched on the end of the bed, and folded her legs up under her nightgown. "It was luck as much as anything. I had no idea where you were this year. And I wasn't ready to entrust all my hard work to the War Office with the hope that they could find you. I thought you might write for Christmas, and I'd know your location then."

He lifted the lid of the box, to reveal neatly wrapped packages resting on a bed of white linen. "New shirts," he said with transparent pleasure. "Bless you. I always had the softest shirts in the regiment."

She'd sewn, washed and bleached each shirt with just that object. The way she had for the last seven years. "I hated to think of you over there with scratchy linen."

"All made by you?"

"Yes." Every stitch a silent declaration of love.

"Thank you." When he lifted one of the smaller packages, a piece of greenery fell from the wrapping. "Mistletoe?"

"For Christmas." This year, she'd placed a few mistletoe sprigs in with his present and made a wish for his safe return as she did it.

He smiled. "For kisses."

"For luck." Feeling very daring, she picked up a sprig and held it over his head as she stretched up to kiss him. Only when he drew her closer and the corner of the box bumped her hip did she recall what they'd been doing before pleasure distracted them.

"Edmund..." she protested, as his hand slipped under the top of the nightdress.

"Mmm?"

Heat rippled through her when he squeezed her breast. "Your present?"

"Mmm," he said, nibbling his way down her neck and making every hair on her skin stand up.

"Present..." She sounded less convincing by the second and was almost sorry when he pulled away.

"Stop tempting me." He kissed her with unmistakable purpose, then returned to his gifts. He unscrewed a silver container. "Bonbons."

"In one of your letters, you said you like peppermint."

"I do." He offered her a sweet, before taking one for himself. "Fancy you remembering that."

Felicity remembered every word he'd ever said or written to her. His delight in the sweet made her smile, even as a burst of fresh mint flooded her mouth. The taste, however delicious, couldn't compete with Edmund's kisses.

"Did you make these, too?"

She nodded. "I made everything I could."

"I've married quite the housewife," he said. "Did you always make everything? You never said."

She blushed. Again. "I know it's not very countessish, but I wanted you to receive a Christmas present that came directly from me."

"Thank you. That's what it felt like." His eyes warmed, and he leaned in to give her a kiss sharp with peppermint. "Now what else is in here?"

She sat back and enjoyed his childlike glee as he opened his gifts. The fruitcake. The Christmas pudding. More bonbons. A parcel of recent novels. Pens and writing paper, included purely out of self-interest. Several cakes of the soap she knew he liked. Tonight when she'd lain in his arms, the sandalwood scent had been hauntingly familiar. Handkerchiefs she'd sat up late finishing only last week, when she'd decided to hold onto the box until she had a confirmed address.

He sat back, surrounded by bounty. "You put me to shame."

She smiled, elated with the success of her gifts.

She'd never suspected this boyish side of his nature existed. What a night of revelations this had been.

"I know these last years, you haven't been in a position to buy me presents." She dared to tease him. "Although next Christmas, I'll expect you to start making up for it."

Amusement brightened his eyes to silver. "So you don't want this year's present?"

Surprised, she stared at him. "This year's present?"

Edmund laughed with a light-heartedness she hadn't heard since his return and shifted his gifts aside so he could stand up. Hardly limping at all, he crossed to his valise and was quick to locate what he sought.

As he approached, he held his hands behind his back. "Close your eyes."

She did.

"No peeking. Put out your hands."

She obeyed.

"Closer together. Do you think I bought you an elephant?"

"Edmund," she protested, but she moved her hands together.

He'd given her a horse as a wedding gift. A fine chestnut mare she rode every day. Avid curiosity gripped her. "What is it? A shawl from Spain? Some lace from the Low Countries?"

"Was that what you wanted? If only I'd known."

Keeping her eyes shut, she reached forward into empty air. "You're a beast."

"Undoubtedly." His voice lowered, until it reverberated in her bones. "Happy Christmas, my lovely wife. This is the best Christmas I've ever known, and I hope it's the first of many glorious Christmases to come."

Something in his tone made her open her eyes, despite his strictures not to look. For a lost moment, she stared into features so vivid with feeling that she wondered if she'd misjudged him all these years. Perhaps he did love her.

"Edmund..." she whispered in a completely different tone. Then he placed a flat red velvet case in her hands, and that aching, intimate connection snapped.

His expression was smug. "It's not a shawl."

The case's weight surprised her. "So I gather," she said unsteadily. She'd seen enough of the Countess of Canforth's jewels to guess what was inside.

"Open it." Watching with unwavering attention, he settled against the pillows again. The expectation in his eyes made her smile, even as she regretted the loss of that instant of silent communion. Her hands shook so badly that she couldn't manage the box's clasp.

"Here." Edmund took it from her. With a couple of flicks of his long fingers, he unfastened the lid and lifted it.

Awed, Felicity surveyed the sparkling contents, before she glanced up at her husband. "Goodness gracious."

He looked pleased. "Goodness gracious indeed. I

bought them in Vienna a couple of months ago, and I've been carrying them around ever since. I always had a yen to see my beautiful wife in rubies and diamonds."

"But what rubies." As she lifted the magnificent necklace from its bed of purple silk, her hands still trembled. Edmund had given her a complete parure. Tiara. Two bracelets. Brooch. Earrings. When she held the necklace up to the candlelight, the stones sparkled as if they were alive.

"Do you like it?" he asked, and she caught a flash of uncertainty in his expression. Another of tonight's miracles. She knew him well enough now to recognize his diffidence for what it was.

"How could I not? They're spectacular. I should say that you've been dreadfully extravagant, but I love them too much to object. Instead, I feel completely overwhelmed. And very grateful."

His laugh held a note of relief. "I'm so glad."

Yesterday she would have thanked him with words and a smile, knowing her response was inadequate to the lavish gift. But tonight, she'd put away her inhibitions. She dropped the necklace and launched herself forward, kissing him with unabashed enthusiasm. "Thank you so much. It's the most beautiful gift I've ever received."

Laughing with no hint of constraint, he tumbled her over and returned her kisses. By the time he raised his head, she stared dreamily up at him.

"Thank you. Thank you. Thank you. I love them." *I love you.*

Warm even through the flannel, his hand curved over her breast. "My pleasure."

Felicity fiddled with a curling lock of hair over his ear. "Will you help me put them on?"

Amusement flashed in his eyes. "My darling, you're not dressed for the occasion. Surely you know it's a faux pas, to wear rubies with flannel?"

His darling? "It is?"

"Better to wear rubies naked, than with a nightgown."

"Oh." Her cheeks heated, but she didn't look away from the brazen invitation in his expression. "In that case, you'd better show me how it's done, my lord."

His smile took on a distinctly wolfish tinge. "It's the least I can do, my lady."

CHAPTER SEVEN

*L*ate Christmas morning—very late, Felicity blushed to admit—she returned to Edmund's bedroom to unpack the valise he'd brought home yesterday. Her husband was downstairs in his library. Because it was Christmas Day, he had no plans to work, but she knew he wanted to start settling back into civilian life after all his years in the army.

She was ridiculously dreamy, and her body felt like it had been through a war of its own. She wouldn't have it any other way. Because beneath the weariness and muscles complaining of strenuous use, she glowed with female satisfaction. Twice more in this bed, Edmund had turned to her. Once, after draping her naked body in a maharajah's ransom in rubies, to launch a leisurely seduction that had stretched into fiery hours of pleasure. Then, when the day was well started, they'd come together with a joy that made her feel like she basked in sunlight, despite the snow falling outside. Never again would she question whether her husband wanted her, or that she was incapable of matching him in sensual pleasure.

She hummed "The Sussex Carol" as she placed the bag on the bed and set to sorting out his clothing, putting aside what needed laundering. There was something wonderfully intimate about performing this housewifely task for the man she loved.

The man she hoped might come to love her.

At times last night, she'd wondered if she'd already won that battle. He'd kissed her with such overmastering need and touched her with such poignant tenderness, surely he must already care.

And he'd remained faithful when his need for some human warmth must have been agonizing. Knowing that he'd stayed true made her heart swell with love. This morning, although no vows had been spoken, she felt cherished. For their first full day together in so many years, that was enough.

While she thought about her handsome husband and the marvelous things he made her feel, her busy hands kept sorting and folding. Until under the clothing, she discovered bundles of papers packed at the base of the bag.

Frowning, she drew out a ragged packet, tied with tatty string. She didn't recognize the letters straightaway as hers, because they were torn and charred and black with soot. It looked like someone had deliberately set out to destroy them.

With shaking hands, she pulled out the rest and scattered them over the bed. Most were burned. A quick check proved that some of the letters came from years ago, perhaps from their first months apart.

What on earth could this mean? Had her husband kept the letters because he treasured them? Had they been damaged in some act of war? Surely Edmund had never been angry enough with her to burn her letters. That wasn't the man she knew.

Once, she might have hidden her rising confusion. But since he'd arrived home, she'd trusted her husband with so much. She'd learned things about their life that she'd never known before. Whatever the result, good or bad, she had to find out the truth behind this mystery.

She grabbed a bundle in shaking hands, leaving the rest behind, and ran out of the room and downstairs. When she reached the landing above the great hall, Edmund was crossing the floor below, Digby at his heels. Today her husband's limp was almost unnoticeable.

"Edmund," she called, her voice uncharacteristically high.

"Yes?" He stopped under the extravagant kissing bough and glanced up. His swift smile faltered, and his eyes narrowed on her face. "What is it?"

"I found these." On shaking legs, she descended the

last flight of stairs and held out the tattered packet with an unsteady hand. "I was unpacking your bag."

"Bugger it. I meant to put them away." To her shock, he turned as red as a sunset when he took the letters. Embarrassment? Or guilt? "My fault, really. A soldier knows to have everything stowed when he makes camp."

Felicity curled her hand around the carved griffin on the newel post. "You're not a soldier anymore."

"Yes, I am. I'll always be a soldier." He subjected her to a searching regard. "Now I suppose you've guessed my deep, dark secret."

Yesterday, she'd have let that enigmatic remark go unchallenged. Not now. She'd been reticent once, and paid for it with endless longing. However unpalatable the truth she uncovered, she'd never let reticence poison her life again.

The turmoil inside her roughened her voice as she stepped toward him. "Who burned my letters?"

"Good God, Flick." Looking aghast, he reached for her arm, but she wrenched out of the way. "What in Hades are you thinking? Whatever it is, it's utterly muddle-headed."

"I can't believe it was you."

"Of course I didn't bloody burn them." He slid the packet of letters inside his coat, as if shielding them from her. "If I did, why the hell would I carry them around as my most precious possession? Stop this."

His most precious possession? If that was true, how

did her letters end up in such a sorry state? She sucked in a shaky breath. "Please…just tell me what happened. I won't be angry."

He lunged forward and grabbed her hard by the shoulders. Obstinacy hardened his jaw in a way that alarmed her. "God, give me strength."

A reckless glitter lighting his eyes, he tugged her forward and kissed her hard and thoroughly under the mistletoe bough. He wasn't hurting her, but his lips were fierce, and his touch was adamant.

Confused, unsure, she struggled to pull away. "Let me go," she muttered under his lips.

"Never," he said, lashing his arms around her in a bear hug.

Gradually his touch eased, until he cradled her in his arms, and he no longer demanded she kissed him back, come hell or high water. Instead his lips wooed, beseeched, coaxed. His warmth enveloped her, and his evocative scent filled her senses. He kissed her as if he'd rather die than stop.

Curse him. Mere hours from his bed, she was ripe for more seduction.

With a helpless moan of acquiescence, she curved into him and kissed him with all the unspoken, irresistible love in her heart. When after a long time, he raised his head to stare down at her with dazed gray eyes, she came close to forgetting what brought her here.

"Damn it, Flick, are you ready to listen to me now?"

He was panting, and he couched the question in a low growl.

The letters… Of course, the letters.

She struggled to sound implacable, but her voice emerged as a husky murmur. "It had better be a good story."

He kept hold of her shoulders, but his touch was tender. If she wanted to, she could escape. She found she didn't want to.

He sucked in an unsteady breath. "It's a love story."

Love? She frowned, still lost in a mist of sensuality. "I don't understand."

Edmund sighed and released her, to her regret. "I know you don't. And it's mostly my fault. But I've always been so terrified of my powerful feelings frightening you away, that I've been infernally dishonest with you, my darling."

She liked being his darling. Almost as much as she liked his kisses. However, this didn't sound good. She frowned. "You're not afraid of anything."

His laugh was hollow. "Of course I am. I'm afraid that you'll never love me."

Silence crashed down. Felicity stared into his face, trying to make sense of what was happening. "Edmund—"

He spoke over her. "I told you there was a story. Well, here it is. It starts with a bumptious brute of an army captain, who thinks he has the world at his feet. Then he meets a beautiful, innocent girl at a ball in

London, and he realizes she's the only world he needs. Against all odds, he wins her for his wife, but she's so fragile and fine, he fears that he'll hurt her. He wants her too much, needs her too much...loves her too much."

"My dear..." she started, wondering if she was dreaming. After nearly eight years without him, and then last night's extraordinary pleasure, this gift he offered her seemed too generous, too rich.

He raised his scarred hand. "Let me finish while I still have the nerve to speak. Anyway, back to our two lovers. Before our army captain can work out the best way to proceed, his country sends him hundreds of miles away from his bride. His only contact with her is a string of amusing letters that say nothing about love or longing or loneliness..."

"I didn't know you loved me." Under his intense stare, she trailed off, letting him go on.

"Luckily our hero survives the war to return to his wife, many hard years later. And he finds time has made no difference to his feelings. He loves her just as much and wants her even more. And this time, he can see that she's ready to meet him as an equal."

She blushed as she recalled the morning's activities. "She certainly did that."

"But that makes him even more terrified, because he's as much under her spell as he ever was. And now he's back to his real life, and they have to work out a way to go on together. He's burning up with love for her—how can he bear it if she feels nothing for him, except duty and lukewarm liking?"

Despite the turbulent emotion vibrating in the air between them, she gave a choked laugh, weighted with unshed tears. "After last night, you can never accuse me of being lukewarm." She drew herself up to her full height, as the last of her shyness fell away forever.

Of course she'd tell him she loved him. Very soon. But first she had a puzzle to solve. "So tell me about the letters."

He ran his hand through his hair. "It's no great mystery. Above Vittoria, we got hit by a French cannonade, and everything in the camp caught fire in a flash. I ran back through the flames to save your letters. I couldn't let them burn. They were all I had of the woman I love."

Felicity caught his hands, as her heart dipped with an overpowering mixture of distress and astounded joy. She wanted to berate him for risking his life over something as trivial as a letter. Yet how could she chastise him, when he loved her enough to face that danger?

"That's why your hands are scarred."

"Yes." His fingers curled hard around hers.

"I should have guessed it was something like that." Her voice shook, as she remembered her shock when she found the charred letters. The tears she'd struggled to hold back trickled down her cheeks.

Blazing gray eyes focused on her face. "Flick, could you love me?"

"Could I? I already do. So much." Her tears threatened to turn into a flood. With a tenderness she no longer needed to rein in, she touched his scarred cheek. "I loved you the moment I saw you."

Elation dawned over his features, making him strikingly handsome. "You love me?"

"I always have." This time, the admission came more easily.

"And I love you."

Her laugh contained a crack. "Which makes me very happy."

His laugh was just as shaky. "Oh, my love, what a Christmas."

"Yes, what a Christmas," she whispered, and stepped into his arms under the kissing bough.

Through the thunderous rejoicing in her heart, Felicity felt Digby pressing into her hip. As the kiss heated up, she became vaguely aware that Biddy had come in, probably to announce Christmas dinner.

"Well, Lord above, all my wishes have come true." Biddy's jubilant voice rang out from the other side of the room. "This is the best Christmas present an old woman could ask for. Welcome home, Master Edmund. Welcome home. You're safe and loved, and you never need to stray from home again."

Edmund drew away from Felicity and smiled down into her eyes with such adoration, she felt the winter day turn to midsummer. She wondered how she could ever have doubted that he loved her, even as she marveled that such a wealth of love could exist in the world and belong to her.

"Amen to that, Biddy," Edmund said, without looking away from his wife.

"Amen indeed," Felicity murmured, stretching up to steal another kiss under the mistletoe.

A MATCH MADE IN MISTLETOE

PROLOGUE

Torver House, Dorset, December 1820

Serena Talbot carefully laid her lace handkerchief on the dressing table and pulled back the corners to reveal the fragile green and white sprig sitting in its soft nest. How absurd it was, that her hands were shaking.

When she raised her eyes to the mirror, she read apprehension in the gray depths. "It's only a silly superstition," she whispered to the blond girl staring back at her.

The blond girl in the reflection looked ready to run for her life.

Around her, the huge, old house was quiet, as it wouldn't be quiet tomorrow when the halls echoed with laughter and happy chatter. The guests for the Talbots' annual Christmas house party arrived in the afternoon.

But tonight held only silence and shadows and flickering candlelight. Caught up in the moment, Serena shivered. She felt like the ghosts of a hundred bygone maidens crowded around her. A hundred maidens who over the centuries had done just what she was about to do.

Had all those other girls felt this same aching longing, this same foreboding that they summoned powers beyond their control?

She straightened and cast the figure in the mirror a derisive glance. "Show some backbone, Serena Frances Talbot."

With swift purpose, she lifted the mistletoe she'd plucked from the kissing bough in St. Lawrence's church in the village and slipped it under her pillow. She'd planned this for weeks. Rattle-pated megrims would not stop her from proceeding.

All her life she'd loved Paul Garside, and now she was twenty-one, it was time to do something about it. This Christmas, she'd do everything she could to make sure he proposed and invited her to take up the glorious life she'd always wanted.

Tonight's ritual placed the seal on her plans. With the mistletoe under her pillow, she'd dream of the man she was to marry. And tomorrow, she'd set out to claim her destiny as Lady Garside.

Once before she'd tried this, when she was eighteen and mad for Paul. The embarrassing truth was she dreamed of him all the time—but that night she hadn't. And he'd spent all Christmas making sheep's eyes at Letitia Duggan.

Since then, Serena had recognized that the mistletoe was telling her she wasn't yet ready. But, oh, how ready she was now, three years later. And Paul gave every indication that he agreed. Whenever they'd met in the last few months, he'd paid her flattering attention.

Smiling at the thought of the handsome baronet she loved, she pulled off her dressing gown and slid into bed. She closed her eyes on a prayer for the mistletoe's blessing.

The day was sunny and warm, although in the way of dreams, snow lay thick on the ground. Serena, walking alone along the path to St. Lawrence's, opened the heavy church door that squeaked in her dreams as it squeaked in life, and stepped into the cool, scented dimness of the vestibule. Before her, a tall man in a hat and formal black coat stood with his back to her. Above him hung the kissing bough, a large ball of mistletoe woven with red and gold ribbon and decorated with apples and green holly.

Music played in the distance. Harps and violins.

Happiness flooded her as she paused in the arched entrance. Glancing down, she saw without surprise that she was dressed for her wedding. When she came in, she hadn't been carrying anything, but now she clasped a pretty bouquet of white roses.

With a light step, she walked toward the man who was yet to look in her direction. At her approach, those impressive shoulders straightened. A triumphant smile curled her lips. Everything she'd ever wanted was coming true. At last.

She was to become Lady Garside, wife to wonderful Paul.

Serena extended one hand to touch the man she was about to marry. "Paul?" she murmured, her joy reaching a crescendo along with the music.

Her heart thumped with wild excitement as her bridegroom slowly turned to face her. She raised her eyes to meet a smiling blue gaze.

And everything crashed into disaster.

The man's eyes were dark brown, almost black. Instead of seeing Paul's clean-cut features, she stared aghast into a saturnine face with slashing cheekbones and a broken nose. Thick brows added a devilish air. A sensual, cynical mouth twisted in the mocking smile that always made her itch to slap it away.

"You!" she spat, lurching back.

"Indeed," Giles Farraday, Lord Hallam, drawled.

That deep voice echoed in her ears when she jerked up against her pillows in gasping horror.

What madness was this? She was meant to marry Paul, not his sarcastic, annoying friend, the Marquess of Hallam. Good heavens, she wasn't even sure she liked Giles. She hated how he watched her, as though he saw past her outward poise to the wild, headstrong girl inside. If it was her choice, she wouldn't have him to stay at Torver. But he'd been a regular visitor since his schooldays. And when the young Serena had asked her mother not to invite the quiet, dark-haired boy, she'd promptly received a scolding for lack of charity.

Giles Farraday was an orphan. His parents had died in India, and he had no family to go to at Christmas. He and Paul had been great friends since they'd met at Eton, although she'd never understood why. Paul was beautiful and golden, an Apollo. Giles was dark and difficult, a Vulcan or a Hades. Giles's humor leaned toward the black, while Paul's was unfailingly sunny.

With a choked growl of disappointment and anger, she ripped the mistletoe from beneath her pillow and flung it to the floor.

She should know better than to trust in old wives' tales.

CHAPTER ONE

Serena still felt out of sorts the next afternoon, when the carriages rolled up to Torver House to disgorge the Christmas guests. A fortnight of family and friends and fun lay ahead. Or so she told herself as she trudged downstairs to join her parents on the wide front stairs, where they waited to welcome the visitors. The house was set on a rise above the train of vehicles making their way along the winding drive.

The day was fine and cold, with a pale, wintry sun in a pale, wintry sky. Beside her, her ebullient, gray-haired father was almost incandescent with anticipation. There was nothing Sir George loved better than this yearly gathering of Talbot connections. Serena's mother, a more contained personality than her father, looked equally pleased in her tranquil way.

First to bound up the stairs toward Serena was her

brother Frederick, tall, dark and exuberant like their father. Followed by Serena's older sisters Belinda and Mary with their families, and a horde of aunts, uncles, cousins, and friends.

By the time everyone shifted into the great hall for spiced wine and gingerbread, the air resounded with laughter and squeals of excitement. Gangs of children chased each other through the cavernous room hung with boughs of Christmas greenery, and various dogs added to the mayhem.

Serena found refuge from the cheerful chaos beside the hearth, where the Yule log blazed. Most years, she loved this explosion of life in a house that had become sadly quiet since her sisters married and her brother took up residence in London. But now, a headache nagged at her, and she couldn't help wishing that the children weren't quite so ecstatic to see their cousins.

"Serena, are you all right?" Mary asked, coming up beside her.

Serena forced a smile. "Fine."

Searching gray eyes, so like her own, leveled on her. "You don't seem yourself."

She didn't feel like herself, but even to this, her favorite sister, she couldn't confess the details of last night's unsettling dream. Anyway, what was there to confess?

A footman opened the main doors to some late-comers, distracting Mary. To Serena's relief.

"Ah, here are Paul and Giles," her sister said with transparent pleasure.

Two vigorous young men strode into the crowded hall and stopped beneath the kissing bough suspended near the door. Torver House always set up a mistletoe corner, although the decoration was less extravagant than the one in St. Lawrence's.

In her ears if not in reality, the cacophony receded, and for one breathless moment, Serena observed the new arrivals as if she'd never seen them before. Which was mad, when she'd known Paul since she was a baby, and Giles since eight-year-old Frederick had brought the orphaned marquess home the Christmas after he started at school.

Sir Paul Garside was a sight to set any girl's heart fluttering. The handsomest man she'd ever seen. Tall. Golden. Perfectly turned out in a dark-blue coat that matched his eyes. At ease with his world.

Unwillingly, almost afraid, she let her attention stray to Paul's companion. Dark. Quieter than Paul. Compelling in his self-possession.

Serena had always disbelieved the gossip that painted Giles as the gentleman the London ladies pursued. But even across the vast hall, something hot and dangerous quivered into life inside her when those unreadable obsidian eyes settled on her.

"Serena?" Mary said sharply, shattering her odd reaction. "Are you listening to me?"

Serena's cheeks heated as she met her sister's curious eyes. "Sorry, Mary. I was miles away."

"No doubt dreaming of a June wedding to Paul Garside," her sister snapped.

Serena's blush deepened, and she checked quickly to see if anyone had overheard. "Shh."

Mary rolled her eyes. "Nobody's paying any attention. And what if they are? Your penchant for Paul is no secret."

"Oh, how mortifying," Serena said in horror.

"Well, in the family at least. It's possible Paul doesn't know. Men are always so clueless about things like that."

"I...I like Paul, I always have." Why on earth did that statement convey an edge of desperation?

"Of course you do. He'll make you a wonderful husband. If you mean to catch him, you must know you've got the family's approval."

Serena's annoyance persisted, although she wasn't sure why. "I had no idea my hopes were subject to such speculation."

Mary's laugh was dismissive. "You're mutton-headed if you don't. A couple of years ago, Mamma made us all promise not to mention it, because you're such a contrary creature, you might go off the idea."

Serena's attention returned to Paul. Her father and mother were giving him a rapturous welcome. Odd how difficult it was to resist looking toward his acerbic friend standing beside him, also welcomed, also loved.

"When I was ten years old, I made up my mind to marry him."

"And why not? It will be a marvelous match. We all love Paul."

Why did Mary's chirpy certainty grate? "You make it sound as if we're already engaged."

Mary subjected her to a thorough inspection and finished with a satisfied nod. "You've turned into a bit of a diamond in the last year or so. And the word is that Paul has noticed."

This should be exactly what Serena wanted to hear, especially as she'd always been a harum-scarum disaster, more inclined to climb a tree or play a hectic game of cricket, than sit with her embroidery.

So why wasn't she overjoyed at Mary's praise—and the news that her family approved of her suitor? This niggle of discontent made no sense at all.

Before she could fathom her odd reaction, Paul and Giles approached.

"And here are my two favorite girls." Paul smiled with the brilliance of a man who never doubted his welcome wherever he went. "Mary, you're looking the picture of health. And, Serena, how lovely you are today. If we were under the mistletoe, I'd kiss you."

"You may kiss me anyway." She smiled at Paul and took his outstretched hands. "It's the privilege of old friendship."

Paul bent to kiss her cheek. She waited for the usual thrill at the touch of his lips. But the fleeting contact left her unmoved. Dear Lord, what was wrong with her?

As she drew away, she caught Giles's interested gaze and stupidly, she blushed. The memory of that horrible dream constricted her breathing, so she sounded cursed fluttery as she greeted Paul's friend. "And, Giles, welcome back to Torver. Did you have a good trip up from London?"

"Serena, how cruel." Ironic humor lengthened Giles's lips. "You've known me nearly as long as you've known this vagabond, yet I don't merit the same rights?"

"Same?" Puzzled, she stared up at him. He towered over her, taller than Paul. How had she never noted that before?

A purr of laughter escaped him as he leaned in. "Who needs mistletoe?"

He'd kissed her before in silly Christmas games. Since their first term at Eton, Frederick had invited Paul and Giles to spend school holidays at Torver House. While Giles's visits in recent years had become rarer, he'd never missed a Christmas. He was part of the fabric of her life.

So why did his casual kiss stop the world? At the cool brush of his lips across her cheek, shivery heat rippled through her. She closed her eyes, fighting for balance.

"Serena?" Giles's soft, deep voice—why had she never before recognized its beauty?—seemed to come from far away.

She blinked and with surprising reluctance, stepped apart from him. Another horrid blush stained her cheeks, and she only just stopped herself from raising a hand to touch where he'd kissed her. Her skin burned where his lips had touched.

Drat that dream. It had turned her batty.

Reluctantly, she met Giles's eyes. Dark and somber, they settled on her face. She'd learned through the years that little escaped his penetrating intelligence. The idea of him seeing her confusion made her cringe.

"Welcome home," she stammered, only realizing what she said after the words emerged.

For once, Giles's smile lacked an edge. "Well, that's a nice reception."

She blinked again to bring the bustling room into focus and realized that the whole interaction had lasted mere seconds. Mary and Paul weren't looking at them but discussing some mutual acquaintance.

Still those enigmatic eyes examined her face. She shifted awkwardly from one foot to the other. "I...I meant..."

To her surprise, he touched her cheek with one elegant hand. Mostly Giles kept his distance from her. Gestures of affection were unheard of. "Don't spoil it."

The brush of his fingers was almost as devastating to her composure as his kiss. "Spoil?"

Could she sound any more like a complete ninnyhammer? Paul stood beside her, yet her attention riveted on Giles.

Giles was still smiling with a sweetness she'd never before associated with brooding Lord Hallam. "I've always thought of Torver as my home, presumptuous as that may be."

"What about Lanyon Castle?"

The Marquess of Hallam had vast estates in Devon. She'd never visited them, but Paul and Frederick had spoken with awe of the splendors of the Farraday feudal pile.

"Brr." Giles gave a theatrical shiver. "Just thinking about the place makes me feel like I'm coming down with a cold."

She frowned. He might sound like he was joking, but something in his expression made her wonder if he was. "I've heard it's magnificent."

The irony crept back into his smile, and she found herself regretting the loss of that unsuspected sweetness. "Oh, it's that, all right."

"But not a home?"

"It takes love to make a home."

Before she could question his statement—surely the most astonishing part of what had so far proven an astonishing day—he turned to speak to Belinda and Frederick who had dodged darting attacks from overexcited youngsters to reach the fireplace.

Released at last from his blazing black gaze, Serena took her first full breath since that extraordinary kiss.

When Giles stared at her, she'd felt as though someone tightened a strap around her chest.

What in the name of all that was holy had just happened?

Nothing. *Everything.*

Who knew Giles concealed a romantic streak beneath his cynical hide?

But that wasn't what had made her heart clench with poignant emotion. No, what made her ache was the revelation that beneath his rakish dash, Giles Farraday was lonely.

Giles looked out the window of the bedroom he always used at Torver House and pondered the bleak winter landscape outside. The estate nestled in a pretty valley where a river ran down toward the distant sea.

But that wasn't what he saw, as he stood above gardens and fields, hills and coppices, all bare with the season.

No, his attention was centered on the knot garden directly below, where his best friend walked in the gathering dusk with the only woman Giles had ever wanted. His best friend, who had informed him a week ago that this Christmas, he meant to offer for Serena Talbot and that he had every hope of being accepted.

Of course he did. He'd be a deuced blockhead if he didn't.

The girl had never had eyes for anyone else. And Paul was quite the catch. Rich, handsome, honorable.

And, Giles admitted grudgingly, a damned nice fellow.

There were no impediments to the match. The families were close, Serena would make the perfect chatelaine for Paul's charming Palladian house. After the wedding, she wouldn't even have to move far from the parents she loved. Paul's estates were only several miles away from Torver.

Everyone liked Paul. Damn it, Giles liked Paul. When he didn't want to shoot the lucky sod for crowning a singularly fortunate life with a happy marriage to lovely, ardent Serena Talbot.

The outcome seemed inevitable. Paul and his bride would live a glorious life, and rear a brood of golden-haired children, and enjoy a contented, prosperous, useful future.

Paul was probably suggesting that very future to Serena right now.

Damn. Blast. Hell. Bugger.

Giles sighed and told himself that he'd always known this day would come. She'd never been for him. That had been clear from the first.

When he'd arrived as a grieving, prickly boy, reeling from the loss of his beloved parents, Serena had been wary. As she'd grown up, her patent adoration for Paul meant that in her world, Giles operated as a mere adjunct to his picturesque friend. Nothing much beyond Paul bloody Garside ever registered with her.

Giles's one consolation had always been that while Paul was undoubtedly fond of Serena, his feelings hadn't advanced far past that. It wasn't much of a consolation. Paul had had more than his share of flirtations, but Giles knew that he always meant to please his family and marry the youngest Talbot girl. In recent months, that plan had changed from a duty to a pleasure.

Paul was as susceptible to a pretty face as the next man. This last year, Serena had fulfilled the promise of beauty that Giles had always seen beneath the muddy pinafores and untidy braids.

So this Christmas, the engagement was all set to go forward.

Except...

Except something unexpected had happened downstairs when he'd kissed Serena—a treat he always paid for in nights of restless longing.

Call him an optimistic fool, but he'd swear that for one sizzling moment, she'd looked into his eyes and seen him. Seen him as the man he was, not Paul Garside's shadow.

And he'd wondered. Hell, how he'd wondered.

Then she'd stepped back.

But that fleeting instant gave him hope. At a time when all hope seemed dead.

The quest might be futile. But he very much feared,

however everything fell out in the end, that he meant to challenge his charming, eligible, handsome friend for the prize they both wanted.

Although if the best man won, Giles hadn't a chance in Hades.

CHAPTER TWO

*T*hree days before Christmas, and Serena remained mired in confusion. She should be deliriously happy, and instead, she was more miserable than she'd ever been in her life.

Which made no sense when at last fate granted her dearest wish, Paul Garside courting her. His attentions since his arrival were unfailing, with the emphasis on unfailing.

This afternoon, in a desperate attempt to find a moment's peace from his constant company, she'd slunk away from the house to seek refuge in the cold and empty village church. When just days ago, the idea that she'd want to do anything but bask in his presence would have seemed preposterous.

But she badly needed time alone to think. To remind herself that all her life she'd wanted Paul to pursue her. She should be ecstatic at his interest.

Instead of scared to death.

When the outside door squeaked behind her, she gave a guilty start. Even if she had nothing to feel guilty about. By heaven, she was turning into a bundle of nerves.

Foreboding in her heart, she glanced back from where she sat in the family pew. Several times Paul had tried to corner her, starting with a chilly stroll in the knot garden the day he arrived. She feared he wanted to get her alone so he could propose. And however unlikely the fact, fear wasn't too strong a term for her reaction to that prospect. Just now, she was in too much turmoil to make any decision.

Oh, how she wanted to kick herself.

The new arrival wasn't Paul. But he wasn't much of an improvement. Instead of a tall, fair-haired man, a taller man with dark, sensual features stood in the arched doorway leading through to the vestibule.

"So this is where you're skulking," Giles drawled, sweeping off his hat as he entered the body of the church. He was casually dressed for the country, in a black coat, doeskin breeches and boots. His insolent gait a silent challenge to sanctity, he sauntered up the aisle toward her.

"I'm not skulking," she snapped. Although to her shame, she was. She slumped back into her seat. "Quiet contemplation is appropriate to the season."

"Paul wants to talk to you." Giles paused beside the

pew and regarded her like some curious scientific specimen.

"Oh," she said glumly, but when Giles's eyebrows rose, she straightened and injected false enthusiasm into her manner. "I wonder what he wants."

"Who knows?"

She knew. He wanted her staring up at him with starry-eyed adoration, as he outlined the future that she'd planned all her life. "He didn't say?"

"I didn't ask. Last I saw, he was checking the stables. They were your regular haunt before you became the Belle of Torver."

"The Belle of…" A blush rose. Which was ridiculous. Giles's tone was taunting rather than admiring. "I should go and find him."

But she didn't shift.

Giles did. To her dismay, closer rather than away.

Her heart somersaulted in a most disconcerting manner. Curling her fingers into her dark green merino skirts, she told herself to settle down. She didn't like this odd, prickly awareness of her brother's friend, but she couldn't control it.

Serena wasn't lurking in the church only to escape Paul. These days, Giles Farraday was just as troublesome.

More, curse him.

"Oh, for God's sake, make him put in some work to catch you. He'll savor his victory all the more if he has to make an effort to win it."

Appalled, Serena stared at him, while another blush stung her cheeks. "What did you say?"

"Would you rather play coy?" He opened the gate to the pew and stepped into the small box to sit beside her. Immediately the echoing space of the parish church shrank to suffocating narrowness. Her nincompoop heart performed a drunken jig in her chest.

She scooped in a shallow breath, sharp with frankincense and old, damp stone and made herself speak. "Why on earth does everyone think I've set my cap at Paul Garside?"

With a mocking smile, Giles put his hat on the seat beside him. "Dear me, I have no idea."

His sarcasm made her wince. "Hmm."

Blindly she stared toward the altar, decorated for Advent with an embroidered violet cloth and holly wreaths. After a long time—or what felt like a long time—Giles murmured, "There's no need to be reticent. He's well and truly reconciled to being caught."

She wanted to tell this overweening lout to mind his own business, but to her surprise she responded honestly. "That's easy for you to say."

Giles's expression was unreadable. She should be used to that by now. "Trust me."

Serena told herself not to respond. She'd said enough. More than enough. Giles and she had never been confidants. In fact, however constant a presence he'd been in her life, they'd never progressed much beyond wary acquaintances.

But some imp inside her remained determined to pursue this mortifying conversation. "I'd...I'd like to think he might do at least some of the chasing."

"Just as a matter of pride."

"Exactly."

Characteristic irony twisted his lips. "I'm sure a clever girl like you can snare a fellow who's already set on having you."

Self-derision edged her laugh. "Then you have more faith in me than I have. When it comes to feminine wiles, I'm a complete novice. Whereas you two have spent the last few years playing the rake in London."

Amusement lit Giles's dark eyes. "I take umbrage at that."

"I can't see why. It's true."

"And how the devil do you know that?"

"Frederick is indiscreet in his cups."

His laugh brushed across her skin like velvet and made every fine hair stand up. "Damn."

"Paul is used to sophisticated women." As her blush heated to fire, she squared her shoulders. She may as well finish this awful discussion. Retreat no longer seemed like an option. "I've never even kissed anyone."

Giles appeared almost as shocked at her confession as she was that she'd made it. Fleetingly he stopped looking like Lucifer sulking in the underworld, and instead became the boy who was a mere five years older than she was. "Serena..."

"There. Now you know the dreadful truth."

Giles had always been something of a mystery to her—this was the longest time they'd ever spent alone together—but his reaction now was particularly cryptic. His marked eyebrows drew together, more in consideration than disapproval, she thought. "You know, perhaps I could help."

Her lips turned down. "How?"

She had the uncanny feeling that he waged some battle with himself. When he met her eyes, she drowned in the dark depths. "I could show you how to kiss a man."

Serena hardly heard. Blood pounded in her ears, and she felt giddy. She had the oddest urge to lean forward and rest her head on that broad chest. Just rest.

Which was mad, when Giles had always been too disagreeable and difficult to be a comfortable companion.

"I'm sorry." Avoiding her eyes, he picked up his hat. "I shouldn't have suggested it."

"Suggested what?" She blinked, forcing herself back to the real world where she wanted Paul, and Giles was just an annoying interloper. "I didn't hear you."

"Oh."

"So what did you say?"

When the raffish Lord Hallam turned charmingly sheepish, her heart performed another of those bewildering little skips. "I offered to be your tutor, to help you cultivate the skills to bewitch the gallant Sir Paul."

"Tutor?"

"I offered to kiss you."

Her heart slammed to a stop.

Good heavens above. Giles was talking about kissing her. How astonishing.

She should be offended. Or angry. Instead the idea lodged in her mind, and wouldn't shift.

The more she thought about it, the more appealing it became. Would it really be so disgraceful to kiss Giles? Serena had long been curious about what a kiss was like. She'd always imagined Paul would be the first man to kiss her. But it might be best to get her clumsy first attempts out of the way with someone whose approval didn't matter quite so much.

Perhaps this was the meaning behind that bizarre, unsettling dream. That Giles was to be her path to Paul. If she'd stayed in the dream longer, maybe Paul would have appeared to oust Giles from the central role.

"Here?" She glanced around the empty church, decorated with green boughs and walls of memorials to long-dead Talbots.

Wonder lit his face. "You agree?"

"Yes, I think I do," she said thoughtfully. "I have a feeling you're quite good at kissing."

A tilt of those expressive eyebrows. "Only quite good?"

Some hitherto unrecognized female instinct was convinced that if Giles set his mind to the task, his kisses would burn her to ashes. But that same instinct warned against sharing that insight. "Don't push your luck."

With a grunt of laughter, he stood. "Never."

She frowned up at him. He was so tall, taller than Paul or Frederick, who were both at least six feet. As a boy, he'd been all gangling awkwardness, hands and feet too big for his lanky limbs. A nose too large for his face. And those swarthy, heavy features were too striking for a child to carry with any conviction.

But somewhere in the last few years, he'd grown into all that character and strength. For the first time, she understood why the London ladies were mad for him. He'd never be classically handsome but, by God, he was interesting and vivid and compelling.

"Giles, if you were teasing about teaching me how to kiss, I'll never forgive you."

"Perish the thought." Attractive self-mockery twisted those full lips. "How the devil can I resist turning you into another man's dream lover?"

Dream lover...

Memories of that disturbing dream washed over her again. Staring at Giles, Serena had a sudden discomfiting suspicion that, despite knowing him most of her life, she didn't really *know* him. And that accepting amorous lessons from him mightn't be altogether wise.

The cynical tinge faded from his smile. "Second thoughts?"

CHAPTER THREE

Serena sucked in a deep breath of cold ecclesiastical air and told herself not to be a ninny. She always responded to a challenge—and the idea of kissing Giles was sinfully appealing. "I'd be a fool not to take advantage of your expertise."

Unholy delight lit Giles's dark face to flashing brilliance. She realized that while he mightn't be handsome, he was breathtakingly attractive and brimming with potent masculinity more powerful than mere good looks.

"Consider me at your service, Miss Talbot." He extended his hand toward her. "Shall we go?"

She took his hand and started when the contact burned, even through his fine leather gloves. Her heart leaped about like a March hare, and anticipation fizzed in her veins. "Go?"

He cast a cool eye around the cavernous church.

"Your illustrious ancestors are making me deuced self-conscious."

She and Giles couldn't stand in the middle of St. Lawrence's and do naughty things to one another. What had happened to her brain? "So where?"

He tipped his chin toward the doorway. "That's a very fine kissing bough in the vestibule."

"Yes, there is," she said shakily, as the ghost of her dream stirred anew. The mistletoe that had caused all the trouble came from that kissing bough. "The vicar doesn't altogether approve of a pagan symbol in a Christian domain, but the villagers would throw rocks through his stained glass windows if he banned the tradition."

"I'm all for tradition." Giles drew her down the center aisle and through the doorway to the narrow room marking the boundary between the church and the outdoors. A shadowy domain between the sacred and the profane, where worshippers could pause to remove their coats and gather their thoughts. And at Christmastime, a place for village lads and maidens to steal a kiss or two.

As Giles positioned her under the pretty ball of ribbons and greenery, Serena shivered with a mixture of dread and tremulous excitement.

"Are you cold?" he whispered, although there was nobody to overhear them.

Yes. No. It was colder here than in the body of the

church—and that had been like an Eskimo's kitchen. "I'm…nervous."

He stepped back and observed her dispassionately, as if checking to see if a painting was straight. "I promise this won't hurt."

She shifted from one foot to the other. It might be lily-livered to confess it, but she felt much braver when he touched her. "That's not why I'm nervous, and you know it."

Unexpected and breathtaking tenderness tinged his smile. "You can change your mind."

Serena straightened and tried to sound nonchalant, but her voice emerged as a croak. "If I deny a kiss under the mistletoe to anyone who requests it, I won't get married next year."

He tugged off his gloves and slid them into his pocket. Something about the deliberate action made her shiver again. "Is that so?"

"Yes," she said on a thread of sound. "In Torver, we're very serious about our superstitions."

"Superstitions are dangerous things."

After her unacceptable dream, nobody knew that better than Serena. "They are."

"In that case, I shouldn't tempt fate." He caught her hand and placed a kiss on her knuckles. A thrill jolted her, even as he released her and crossed to shut and bolt the door to the outside.

Good heavens, he looked like he meant business. How daunting. How…intriguing.

She couldn't take her eyes off him. Had his walk always been a tiger's prowl? How had she missed that Giles Farraday oozed sexual confidence?

"What if someone wants to use the church?" she asked shakily.

"They can come back later."

Serena wanted to ask how much later, but her courage failed. In fact, fears the size of monster frogs performed acrobatics in her stomach. As if observing herself from a distance, she wondered why she didn't run off shrieking. But however frightened and unsure she was, an army couldn't drag her away.

Giles returned to stand before her, cradling her head between his hands. "Are you ready for your lesson?"

His hands were warm and gentle against her hair. She gulped for air, but it did nothing to soothe her nervousness. "I…I think so."

"I have a feeling you're going to prove an excellent student."

"I wish I did," she admitted.

His laugh was soft. "Don't worry. You're in safe hands."

And the lunatic truth was she absolutely believed that.

Giles leaned in slowly, she suspected to give her time to back out of their arrangement. But curiosity remained her most powerful reaction. She was desperate to discover what a kiss was like.

No, it was worse than that. She was desperate for Giles Farraday to kiss her.

His breath brushed across her lips, awakening tingling sensations all over her body.

When still she didn't shift away, his lips skimmed hers with an inquiry that shuddered through her like cannon fire. She closed her eyes, and a hum of welcome escaped her.

Giles's lips settled and moved on hers. Gradually the shock faded, and Serena became aware of details beyond his overwhelming nearness.

His scent. Fresh as snow, although no snow had yet fallen. The touch of his hands on her head. The strength he held in check. His beckoning warmth.

That intimate, unforgettable contact of mouth on mouth.

She started to sway, and the world turned red at the edges. But when Giles withdrew at last, she ached to call him back. Her hands fisted in her skirts as she fought the urge to grab him and haul him close. She prayed that her rubbery legs would hold her up.

"Breathe, Serena," he murmured. "For God's sake, breathe."

She opened dazed eyes to find him regarding her with a quizzical expression. Through her giddiness, she realized she hadn't drawn a breath since the kiss began. When she inhaled, the pain in her lungs and the thickness in her head eased.

"That was…interesting," she stammered.

"Only interesting?" He released her and stepped back. "I must be losing my touch."

"Nice," she said quickly, although that was an inadequate description for those turbulent seconds when his lips met hers.

He burst out laughing. "Is that the best you can do?"

She'd imagined thunder and lightning, something to change her life forever. Kissing Giles had made her blood swirl with muddled longing, but it hadn't set her world alight. "Enlightening?"

"Hmm."

"Inoffensive."

He groaned theatrically. "My vanity will never recover."

"Look, I know you're doing me a favor." Serena glared at him and remembered why she'd spent much of her girlhood wanting to shove Giles Farraday into the nearest puddle. "I'm grateful. Of course I am. But I expected…more."

Her fumbling explanation didn't meet with his approval, she could see. He returned to studying her as if she belonged to some unidentified species. "What kind of more?"

She hissed with frustration. Frustration with him, and with the dissatisfaction curdling her stomach. "I don't know. You're the blasted libertine. You tell me."

"Perhaps the fault lies with you—I'm unaccustomed to kissing ladies who do their best to imitate a block of wood," he said lightly.

Stabbing hurt prompted an incoherent protest. "That's not fair. I told you I'd never done this before."

With unconcealed displeasure, he folded his arms and surveyed her down that long, crooked nose. "I hoped some natural instincts might kick in."

"Perhaps my natural instincts only work when my affections are engaged," she retorted.

Those fearsome brows lowered over glittering dark eyes. If she hadn't been so het up, she might have been afraid. "What the hell is that supposed to mean?"

She put her hands on her hips and drew herself up to her full height, frantic to claim every inch she could against him. "If Paul kissed me, I'm sure I'd get into the spirit of things."

Chagrin flashed in his face, and if he'd been a different, less self-sufficient man, she might wonder if she'd hurt his feelings as he'd hurt hers. "If that's so, by all means go and kiss Paul. But remind him to bring a muffler and some thick socks so he doesn't get frostbite."

She faltered back with a cry. "That's cruel."

He sighed and ran his hand through his hair. "It was. I'm behaving like a brute." The anger drained from his face. "I'm sorry, Serena. For your first kiss, that was a creditable effort."

She frowned, her own anger receding. Grudgingly she admitted that she'd been ungracious first. "No, it wasn't."

"Still, I had no right to be unkind."

Her arms flopped down by her sides in a gesture of defeat. "Perhaps I'm just no good at kissing." She started to turn away, misery tugging at her. "I'm sorry for bothering you—and for being so rude. I'm sure with a more promising candidate, your kisses are perfectly lovely."

"Hold on." He caught her arm and despite everything, heat zapped along every nerve. "Don't give up so fast."

Puzzled, she faced him. "Why on earth would you want to try again?"

"I hate to leave a job half-finished."

His earnestness summoned a bleak laugh. "Very commendable."

"I'm game if you are."

She straightened and narrowed her eyes at him. "I'm always game."

Serena waited for him to deride her bravado, but he gave her another of those uncommonly sweet smiles. "I know you are. I've always admired your courage."

In all their years of acquaintance, he'd never given her a compliment. Before she could muster a response to that astonishing statement, he set her back beneath the kissing bough.

She twined her hands at her waist and stared at him, troubled. "Perhaps it would help if you don't rely on my instincts, and you tell me what to do."

"You hate people telling you what to do."

That was, unfortunately, true, although she'd never

imagined Giles had paid her enough attention to notice. What a day of surprises this was. "Today I bow to your prowess."

"Thank you," he said with a hint of familiar irony. He caught her restless hands. "First, let's put these somewhere useful."

When he placed one hand on his shoulder, she started to draw away. After the kiss, touching his shoulder shouldn't matter, but there was something fiercely unsettling about having her hands on him. "Is it necessary to touch you?"

"Definitely." He replaced her hand where he'd set it. Then he caught the other. "Now where to put this one?"

"Giles…" she said in warning.

He ignored her repressive tone and curved her arm around his back, forcing her closer. "Here, I think, for the moment at least."

She was painfully conscious of the powerful male form mere inches away. The rest of the church might be bitterly cold, but under the kissing bough, sultry summer ruled. "What do I do now?"

"Stare into my eyes as if it would kill you to look away."

"I only want to learn how to kiss," she muttered, directing her gaze everywhere but at him. If she obeyed, he'd guess that her heart raced with forbidden excitement.

"No, you want to learn how to capture a man's attention and keep it. Kissing's just part of the game."

She wanted to argue, but he was right. Blast him. The most terrifying part of this terrifying encounter was that just now, the man she wanted to attract was standing in front of her. And that was completely insupportable.

"Look at me, Serena," he said in a deep voice she'd never heard before.

This time, she couldn't deny him. She raised her chin and stared into those dark eyes. Who knew a man's eyes could be so fascinating? As the silence extended, her head started to swim. After last time, she knew enough to snatch a breath before she lost her balance.

It didn't help.

For the first time, she saw Giles Farraday in full. And heaven help her, the view was magnificent. Without prompting, her hand slid up his shoulder and around his neck, until his black curls brushed her fingers.

"Very good," he whispered. "Now move closer."

He didn't need to tell her. Already she swayed forward, as if he was the moon and she was the tide. When those thin, elegant hands closed around her waist, heat sizzled through her.

"Don't jump, girl," he murmured. "None of this should come as a surprise. You know he wants to touch you. He can't do anything else."

She barely heard as she tilted her face up. "Giles…"

"Yes, like that." Impossibly his dark gaze turned darker. "As if you can't endure waiting one more second for him to kiss you."

Rising on her toes, she stretched toward those beguiling male lips. "You're talking too much."

Still he held apart. Curse him. Did he mean to drive her mad? "Now you're getting the idea."

"Kiss me," she whispered.

"Excellent." Except he no longer looked in charge. Instead he looked as dazed as she felt.

"Kiss me, Giles."

One more excruciating second of delay, before his grip on her waist tightened with unmistakable purpose. "Damn it, Serena," he groaned as his mouth crashed down on hers.

CHAPTER FOUR

Through the rush of blood to his head, Giles heard Serena's shocked gasp. Before he could tell himself to move away, to treat her with the respect she deserved, she curved so close that he felt every inch of her warm, lovely body.

Ridiculous that in all his years of fantasizing about kissing Serena Talbot, Giles had never imagined that he'd ever have the real woman trembling in his arms. Yet as she pressed against him with such eagerness, waves of shivering combed through her.

It was poignantly moving to know that he was the first man to taste those luscious pink lips. He took his time, letting her grow accustomed to the kiss. Yet still the doors of heaven remained closed against him. Although at least now, she made some attempt to join in. Greedy hands closed around his arms, and her lips moved with subtle interest against his.

Too subtle.

He trailed his lips along her cheek, and his hold on her waist firmed. Essence of Serena filled the air. Flowers. Lemon soap. A tinge of feminine warmth that was new.

"Open your mouth, Serena," he murmured.

She started with surprise. "Open? That seems…odd."

He smiled and nuzzled her silky hair, tied up in its usual loose knot. If fate ever granted him a moment's true privacy, he'd tug every pin free, until that golden mass cascaded over his hands.

"I know what I'm doing."

"I don't," she said shakily.

Despite her fears, she turned to glance her mouth across his with a beguiling mixture of hesitation and boldness. His heart crashed against his ribs. Heat seared away all thought of where he was, including the knowledge that the village church wasn't the most discreet site for a tryst.

Their lips, barely parted, clung, and he tasted her sweet, humid breath. He slipped his tongue into the honey interior, letting her rich flavor flood his senses.

She made a soft sound—protest or acceptance, he couldn't say. Then with beguiling enthusiasm, she angled up, and her mouth flowered under his. He tasted her deeply, as darkness invaded his head and desire gushed through his veins.

Serena was delicious, glorious, marvelous. Better than his dreams.

Her tongue fluttered against his, and it was his turn to groan in wordless encouragement. The kiss took fire, and he caught her up against him, lashing his arms around her, wishing to hell that he never had to let her go. A tiny glimmer of reason warned him that he went too far, too fast.

The angels who watch over foolish girls too trusting for their own good must have been listening. He became aware of a sound that didn't belong in this paradise.

Serena must have heard it, too, because she stiffened without, he was pleased to note, moving away. "Some-one's trying to get in," she said on a mere breath of sound.

"I locked it. I told you," he said into her ear and couldn't resist biting her earlobe.

"Giles…" she protested on a sensual shiver. "People will talk."

"Let them. Nobody knows who's in here."

The heavy iron handle rattled again, then fell silent. Serena stared up at Giles with an expression he couldn't read.

"See?" he murmured. "I said they'd go away. Shall I kiss you again?"

A pretty blush, visible through the gloom, colored her cheeks. "You know, I've never really…seen you before."

Satisfaction flooded him. What a long way they'd come in an afternoon. For once, she wasn't thinking about Paul. She was thinking about Giles Farraday.

How could he bear to send her away? He might go back to being invisible.

But they'd dared enough, even if his needy soul wanted to seize her and keep her forever. He was reluctantly loosening his grip, just as the unthinkable happened.

"Serena?"

Hell's bells. Paul's voice emerged from behind the wall separating the vestibule from the body of the church. When he couldn't open the main door, he must have come in through the vestry at the back.

"Oh, Hades in a cookpot," Serena whispered, her horrified gaze clinging to Giles.

"Serena, are you in here?"

"I should have locked the other door, too, damn it," Giles muttered.

In the bristling silence, he heard the click of Paul's heels down the aisle toward them. Serena grabbed Giles's hand and hauled him toward a large oak settle with high sides. A place for pallbearers to catch their breath. Or a guilty lover to hide.

Taking Giles with her, she squeezed into the narrow gap between the side of the seat and the wall. The space was restricted. Delightfully so. Although with discovery so close, he was a cad to notice. Her bosom pressed into his waistcoat, and he had to lean away to conceal his sexual excitement.

"Serena?" Paul's voice grew louder as he approached.

"Dear heaven." She hid her face in Giles's neck. His hold tightened, and he kissed the top of her head in reassurance.

"Stay here," he whispered.

"No…"

"Trust me," he mouthed, untangling her frantic fingers from his shirt.

When she nodded, he brushed a final kiss across her lips. If Paul saw Serena's pink cheeks and swollen lips, he'd know exactly what she'd been up to. Even without Giles's incriminating presence.

He paused long enough to straighten his clothes and check all his buttons were done up. Nothing was out of place. Things were starting to get interesting when Paul turned up. Curse him.

Giles slipped across to the door and released the latch, making no attempt to muffle the noise the heavy iron fittings made.

"Serena?" Paul appeared on the worn stone step leading from the church down to the vestibule. "Oh, it's you, Giles. How did you get in? The door was locked when I tried it."

"Dashed odd. I had no trouble with it." Out of the corner of his eye, he watched Serena shrink into the shadows beside the settle.

"Have you seen Serena?" At least Paul didn't sound suspicious. Yet. "Frederick said he saw her heading this way."

"I ran into her in the garden, and she said something about checking on her horse." Struggling for a relaxed manner, Giles moved past his friend into the church. He wanted to get as far as he could from that blasted kissing bough.

Instead of following, Paul planted his feet on the step and frowned into the vestibule. "I tried there."

If the blockhead veered one inch to the left, the game was up. Giles's gut tightened in dread. He'd never meant to risk Serena's reputation.

"It's a cold day." Giles crossed into the side aisle, hoping Paul would follow. "She might be in the library. A parcel of books arrived from Hatchards yesterday, and I know she's keen to read the latest Walter Scott."

"I tried there, too."

"Well, devil if I know where the chit is. She's obviously not here. Let's go back to the house and ask."

"So you haven't seen her?"

"If I had, I'd tell you." *Liar. Liar. Liar.*

The beginnings of doubt entered Paul's eyes. "It seems odd to find you in a church, when you don't have to be."

True. Which said a little too much about the state of his soul. "Thought I'd take a look at the family memorials."

Paul's puzzled frown deepened. "You've never been interested in ancient monuments."

Paul was no fool, although right now Giles dearly wished he was. He mustered a nonchalant shrug. "I wanted a walk, and I wandered in here to satisfy idle curiosity. It's not worth fighting about."

Paul settled a narrow-eyed gaze on him, and briefly Giles wondered if his interest in Serena was quite as secret as he imagined. "So you're perusing Latin inscriptions?"

"Well, I meant to, until you ruined my contemplative mood. Come on, old man. It's perishing in here."

He prayed his humorous impatience would stop Paul staring into the vestibule, as though Serena was about to jump out of the woodwork. The damnable fact was that she just might.

Instead of cooperating, Paul's gaze swept the shadowy space, and for a horrible moment, his attention settled on the heavy oak settle.

Giles's heart surged into his throat. Good God, he'd marry Serena tomorrow. Today, if he could. But he didn't want her hurt or shamed—and undoubtedly if Paul discovered her in this compromising situation, she'd be both shamed and hurt.

Not sure whether he was a hero or a numbskull, Giles headed toward the back of the church, hoping Paul would follow.

He didn't. "Why not the front door?"

Damn, why not the front door? Giles slammed to a

halt before a memorial under a stained glass window depicting the Prodigal Son. Given the loss of his parents—they'd died in an epidemic in India the year he started at Eton—that particular parable had always touched him. Since his parents' death, unconditional love had been absent from his life. "This very fine example caught my eye."

To his relief, Paul at last wandered over to stand beside him. His friend leveled a long look at the memorial to Obadiah Talbot, who gave his life for king and country at the Battle of Malplaquet a hundred years ago. "I had no idea you'd become a blasted antiquarian."

"It's a recent interest," Giles said lightly, as he conducted a frantic search for something on the marble plaque worthy of comment. Perhaps a genuine enthusiast would commend it. A mere layman couldn't for the life of him discern anything noteworthy in old Obadiah's laconic epitaph.

"Funny you never mentioned it."

Yes, that was funny. Deuced odd, in fact.

"I feared you'd mock me." He assumed a disappointed expression. "And I was right."

"So what's so special about this one?" Paul folded his arms and regarded Giles with a skeptical eye. "Looks dull as damned ditchwater to me."

Looked damned dull to Giles, too. "But you're no connoisseur, are you?" He struggled manfully on. "The elegant simplicity of the carving makes this an exceptional example."

"Is that so?"

"Indeed. The plain square shield and unadorned text combine in a moving memorial to a brave man who died far from home."

Paul continued to sound unconvinced. "If you say so, chum. Although the family story is that old Obadiah was stabbed in a brawl in a brothel the night before the battle. That's why not much fuss was made of his memorial. He was always a bad 'un."

Wouldn't you know it? Bloody Obadiah.

Desperate to avoid Paul's searching regard, Giles headed for the vestry. "I'll still raise a glass in his honor, when we get back into the warm. If Serena has an ounce of sense, she's in the house, toasting her toes by the fire."

Paul shot one last look around the empty church, despite it being conspicuously Serena-less, and shrugged. "I may as well search for her there as anywhere, I suppose. The chit's been dashed elusive since I arrived."

Now that was much more interesting than a memorial to some disreputable Talbot. "She's helping her mother manage a house full of people. I wouldn't take it personally."

"I don't."

Giles burned to pound away Paul's smug smile. Of course he didn't take it personally. Serena had always been under his thrall.

So where did that leave that interloper Giles Farraday, Marquess of Hallam? Out in the cold? Or promising to change from the race's dark horse to hot favorite?

Before those kisses, he wouldn't have wagered a groat on his chances. Now? Now he wondered who she'd been thinking about when his tongue had been in her mouth. The man she dreamed of? Or the one who woke her to sensual pleasure?

He'd give half his considerable fortune to find out.

CHAPTER FIVE

he remnants of fear bitter as bile on her tongue, Serena heard Giles and Paul leave through the back of the church. She remained hidden where she was, grateful for Giles's quick thinking, although she couldn't imagine anyone crediting that he'd become a specialist in church architecture. Now she'd sampled his searing kisses, the idea seemed almost blasphemous.

Only as her heart slowed and her terror of discovery receded did she have a chance to wonder at her reaction to Paul's arrival—and to Giles's kiss.

How interesting that not even a girl in love with another man could resist a rake's wiles. Clearly Giles had learned a lot from the worldly London ladies. The first kiss had been pleasant, but once he'd enlisted her participation, the results had been extraordinary, an emotional flight way beyond the mere physical. And the physical had surpassed anything she'd ever known.

If she felt like that with a man she barely liked, imagine how she'd feel when Paul kissed her.

Except her first reaction when Paul interrupted the shameful experiment—they were in a church, for heaven's sake—had been annoyance. She'd wanted him to go away, so she could go back to kissing Giles.

That didn't seem right. Just as the way the sinful heat lingered in her blood didn't seem right either.

Giles Farraday must be an extremely skilled kisser.

A wanton question arose, before she remembered that it was Paul she wanted. What else might Giles teach her?

Torver House was crammed to the rafters with Christmas cheer—and Giles had slunk away like a guilty man to sit beside the library fire, desperate to escape the jollity. Apart from him, everyone was in a party mood. There were games in the drawing room, and dancing in the great hall. With the family reunited to celebrate the season, dinner had been uproarious.

From the first, Giles had enjoyed staying with the Talbots. They welcomed him with a generosity that he'd always known was exceptional.

But envy tinged his gratitude. Because however kind this noisy, loving, exuberant clan was, however willingly they included him in their festivities, he remained an outsider.

An outsider yearning after the lovely daughter of the house like grim Hades yearned after bright Persephone. Darkness hungering for irresistible light.

If Serena and Paul reached an understanding this Christmas—and why the hell shouldn't they?—Giles would have to stop visiting Torver. Not only would he lose the girl he loved, he'd lose the closest thing he had to a family.

The future looked mighty bleak.

He was hunkered down in here because he couldn't endure seeing Paul and Serena dancing together, beautiful and golden, and from an easier, warmer world than the one Giles Farraday inhabited. If he felt that way now, how the devil would he survive knowing that every night, those two golden beings lay in each other's arms?

With a closed fist, he thumped the arm of his leather chair. And wished to God that he was thumping his best friend.

Love was purgatory. He wished it to the devil.

After this afternoon's antics in St. Lawrence's, his misery bit sharper than ever. He'd felt so clever coaxing his luscious darling into kissing him, but now he paid for his sins. Because his dreams at last moved into the realm of reality, the pain of knowing Serena would never be his was sharper than ever. Tonight he knew what it was to hold her and drink in her scent and hear her sighs of pleasure.

All evening, he'd burned to touch her again. While she skipped about in Paul's arms as if she hadn't a care in the world. Clearly she spared no thought for dark, brooding, lonely Giles Farraday.

With a muffled groan, he raised his brandy glass to his lips, appreciating the liquor's burn down his throat. He was sick to the stomach of his festering self-pity.

When the library door eased open, Giles glanced up from the old "Blackwood's Magazine" that he made a show of reading. If Paul intruded upon his sulks, he might just punch that handsome nose.

But it wasn't his best friend who edged into the room. Instead, it was the lovely girl who had fueled years of dreams and who kept Giles returning to Torver House, no matter how wretched it made him.

The stark truth was that however wretched he felt with Serena, he felt more wretched away from her.

"Giles?" With a furtive air, she shut the door behind her.

The huge library suddenly seemed as small as a shoebox. Just what was she up to?

"I thought you were busy dancing." As he set his brandy aside, he cursed the remark's snide note. But he felt like a dog chained and left to starve.

"I was." With tendrils of hair escaping the loose knot and a flush of exertion in her cheeks, Serena looked utterly beguiling. Dances at a Torver Christmas included vigorous country reels and jigs, as well as measures fashionable in high society. "Why didn't you stay? I wanted to dance with you."

"Trying to make Paul jealous?" In a spurious attempt at insouciance, he stood and leaned one elbow on the mantelpiece. "Good move. Machiavellian. At this rate, you won't need too many more lessons before you've mastered the game of flirtation."

When her gray eyes darkened with hurt, he wanted to kick himself. It wasn't her fault that she preferred another man. During those rare moments when he rose above his jealousy, he could even admit Paul had every chance of making her happy.

"You're being horrid. Why?"

Because he struggled to preserve a scrap of pride when he teetered on the edge of humiliation. But that didn't mean she deserved his spite. "I'm sorry. A case of the seasonal megrims."

Serena studied him with a troubled expression, her hands loosely linked at her waist. She wore a light blue dress in some floaty material that made him think of summer instead of the depths of winter. "Will you come back and dance with me?"

Stand before all the people he loved and pretend he felt nothing stronger than mild friendship for Serena Talbot? He'd rather have all his teeth knocked out with a hammer. "I don't like dancing."

His surliness should chase off a sensible girl. Clearly

Serena wasn't sensible. She drifted further into the room, curse her. "You used to."

"I've changed."

"That's true." The color in her cheeks intensified. "You've grown very handsome."

Heat turned his own cheeks red. And didn't that make him a soppy sod? In London, he did a fair job of playing the man of the world. Here with Serena, he felt like the awkward schoolboy who had arrived at Torver eighteen years ago. "Doing it too brown, Serena. I've always been an odd-looking beggar."

"You certainly were as a boy." To his surprise, fondness curved her lips. "Nothing seemed to fit. Your nose was too large, your legs were too long—"

"My feet were too big."

"Yes. Yet even then, you danced."

He shot her a narrow-eyed look. "What's this about, Serena? Requests for my company. Compliments on my appearance. You mean some mischief, or I'm a Dutchman."

Trailing her hand along the edge of a gilt and mahogany table, she stepped closer. Every hair on his body stood up in alarm—and forbidden longing. "I liked what we did this afternoon."

"So did I," he said, before he had a chance to question the wisdom of reminiscing about kisses, when they were alone together and at imminent risk of discovery.

"I'd like another lesson."

Her frankness felt like a punch to the stomach. He straightened and struggled for a coherent reply. "There's no mistletoe in here."

"You could kiss me under the kissing bough in the hall. Nobody would look twice."

A grunt of unamused laughter escaped. "They would, if I kissed you the way I did this afternoon."

She bit her lip. "You could kiss me here and pretend there's mistletoe."

"I thought you were in love with another man." The words felt like a blow to a bruise, but they had to be said.

Instead of taking offense, she stopped at the end of the table and regarded him with an enigmatic expression. Which was odd. He'd spent years observing Serena. He thought he knew her as well as he knew himself.

Tonight proved him wrong.

A prudent man would send her packing. But he'd been hungry for her company for so long, he couldn't yet bring himself to banish her back to the family—and that ass Paul.

"Perhaps I'm flighty."

Another grim laugh. "Not you. You're the faithful type." Unfortunately so was he, damn it. "You've always adored the eligible Sir Paul. You've never wavered."

She looked annoyed. "It's so embarrassing to discover that everybody has been speculating about my affections."

Giles leaned back more naturally, starting to enjoy himself, despite everything. In the long, desolate years ahead, he'd recall every moment of this encounter when Serena had taken the trouble to seek him out. The candlelight on her skin and hair. The distant sounds of the packed house. Having her to himself when for once, she didn't seem to want to be elsewhere.

Even if she still wittered on about Paul Garside.

Oh, well, real life was rarely perfect. Otherwise, how would a man know he'd made it to heaven? "If you mean to turn into a flighty piece, you'll have to learn to dissemble."

"I can dissemble," she said in a cranky voice that made him want to hug her.

By now, she was mere feet away. One small step, and he'd be close enough to touch her.

He stayed where he was. "Not that I've noticed."

"I can learn."

"That would be a pity."

She frowned. "Is that why you won't give me more lessons? Because you think I'll give the game away?"

He shook his head. "No, it's because I'm not sure what you're playing at. I thought I knew, but now I'm puzzled. And I never said I wouldn't give you another lesson."

Her body sagged with relief. He was shocked to realize that whatever went on in that busy mind, she hadn't come after him on a whim. This was important to her. Although for the life of him, he couldn't imagine why. They both knew that she should concentrate on winning Paul, not on kissing Paul's best friend.

"I'm so glad," she admitted. "When you avoided me tonight, I thought I must have done something wrong this afternoon."

"You did. You kissed me when you intend to marry another man." If he kept saying it, he might have some chance of retaining a shred of control.

One pale hand waved in dismissal. "It's in a good cause."

"I doubt anyone else would agree."

"Nobody else has to know. I feared I'd given you a dislike of me. You didn't look at me at dinner." The sweet earnestness in her regard pierced his heart. "And when the dancing started, you scuttled away like a rat from the light."

He snorted in self-derision. "Not flattering."

"But true. So you'll kiss me again?"

"You seem deuced preoccupied with kisses." He bent to stoke the fire. If he kept looking at her, he hadn't a hope in hell of keeping his hands to himself. "I don't want to spoil your chances with Paul."

More lies.

"Perhaps I want to sow a few wild oats before I settle down."

"Respectable ladies don't sow wild oats, my darling."

The endearment slipped out before he could catch

it. As he stood upright, he saw her stiffen, but she still hovered too bloody close.

"Perhaps they should." She tilted her chin with familiar defiance. "I've never felt so alive as I did in your arms. I'm happy you enjoyed it, too."

Giles bit back a groan. "Leave me alone, Serena."

"Why?" She dared another step closer.

His hand closed so hard around the poker that it hurt. "Because anyone could walk through that door."

She looked directly at him, and at last he realized what his habitual self-denial had kept concealed. Although her kisses this afternoon should have hinted that things had changed.

His heart slammed into the wall of his chest. A universe of possibilities opened before him, possibilities a man of honor would resist.

She might love Paul—she *did* love Paul, everyone knew that. But right now, she wanted Giles Farraday.

"I'm not sure I care," she said in a low, urgent voice.

Setting the poker back in the basket, he fought the unworthy impulse to take her at her word. "You would tomorrow."

When he faced her, such disappointment darkened her eyes that he almost abandoned principle and good sense—even the hope of his next breath—to kiss her. To do more than kiss her. But he'd lived with desire much longer than she had. He'd counted the consequences of surrendering to impulse.

That lush mouth turned down in displeasure. "So you won't kiss me?"

"No."

Because he feared where kisses would lead. And he had no right to take that journey with her when scandal loomed so close.

"Ever?"

The blood thundering in his ears made it hard to hear. "What?"

"Will you ever kiss me again?"

Oh, hell. She made a mockery of scruples. "It wouldn't be wise."

She shrugged. "I told you—I'm not going to be wise this Christmas. Will you come riding tomorrow morning?"

He arched his eyebrows. "And find a secluded glade? You're playing with fire, Serena."

Her sensual smile astonished him. She'd come a long way since this afternoon, when she'd stood like a doll and let him lay siege to resolutely closed lips. "I hope so."

"What about Paul?" he asked, as much to remind himself what she had at stake as to stir her conscience.

That delicate jaw firmed into a stubborn line. "Paul takes me too much for granted."

Ah, now he understood. While she might want Giles, this invitation wasn't about him, but about Paul. "So I'm a means to an end?"

"Do you mind?"

He damn well should. He was proud to a fault. As an orphan flung into a ruthless and alien environment, pride had helped him survive. Before answering, he examined his feelings. He should send her away with a flea in her ear and a strict warning about gambling with her reputation.

He should.

Giles spoke slowly. "You know, I'm not sure I do."

Satisfaction glowed in her blue eyes. "So you'll kiss me?"

"Not now."

"Tomorrow?"

In the long run, he'd suffer for this agreement. But how the devil could he resist her? "I'll meet you in the stables at dawn."

"Good." She didn't retreat, although she'd got her way. "Now come back to the hall and dance with me."

He couldn't help smiling. Dear God, she'd been created to torment him. "You're a demanding wench."

"Is that a yes?"

"That's a no."

She raised her arms. "Then dance with me here."

"There's no music."

"I'll hum."

"Serena…" he said helplessly, although he took her hand and slipped his arm around her supple waist.

"A waltz?"

Self-mockery edged his laugh. "What else?"

When Serena sang, he found the husky catch in

each note ineffably moving. As his feet found the rhythm, they moved in perfect time.

He thought he'd been smart to evade another kiss, but this dance proved just as perilous. Especially now he knew how it felt to hold her even closer. He drew her near and tucked her head under his chin. Her flowery scent fed his senses.

"Should you hold me so tight?" she whispered.

"Probably not."

"I like it."

With no music, they faltered to a stop. He rubbed his chin on the soft hair at her crown. "I'm beginning to think that you like a lot of things that aren't good for you."

"Aren't you good for me?" she murmured, and her hand slid along his shoulder to curl around his neck.

Desire surged, hot and invincible. He swallowed to moisten a dry mouth and told himself to push her away.

He didn't.

For a sweet interval, they embraced like lovers.

"Start singing," he growled. "Or take the consequences."

She lifted her head and for one sizzling second, he thought all his dreams might come true. That she'd say she wanted him and not Paul Garside. And that she didn't give a rat's arse if the whole world knew it.

Her eyes flickered down, and she picked up the

inane little tune again. Hesitant, but true. And he went back to circling her around the room.

"So this is where you are," Lady Talbot said from near the door.

Serena gasped and tugged free of Giles. She looked so guilty, one might think she'd been committing murder instead of dancing with an old friend. "Mamma…"

Giles pretended a nonchalance he didn't feel. Over the years, he'd learned a little about dalliance. The appearance of innocence counted for much when caught in a compromising position. "Lady Talbot, Serena was showing me how she waltzes."

Serena's mother, blond and slender like her daughter, leveled an unreadable gaze upon him. "So I see."

Serena had gathered her poise. "Giles was being unsociable, so I came looking for him."

That was true, as far as it went. A girl's mother didn't need to know about kissing lessons and dawn rendezvous.

"It's time you both rejoined the party. We missed you."

Giles heard no hint of criticism, just the acceptance he always received at Torver House. Or, a less welcome theory, perhaps like everyone else, Lady Talbot was so used to her daughter pining after Paul that she saw no harm in Serena dancing with Giles.

Much less welcome.

"Of course, Lady Talbot." He presented his arm to

Serena, but she gave a minuscule shake of her head. He glanced between mother and daughter and made his exit with a bow.

He paused outside, worried that Serena's mother intended to scold. If she did, he'd step in to defend his beloved.

"Mamma, I'm sorry for deserting the party," Serena said.

"No matter, darling girl. It's Christmas, and nobody's standing on ceremony. If you hadn't come to fetch Giles, I would have. He doesn't understand that he's one of the family."

"I really like him, Mamma. Frederick is lucky to have such a friend."

He winced at the word "like." But pique couldn't dampen his gratitude and affection for this remarkable family.

"I've always thought so. Paul arrives sure of a welcome, whereas Giles hangs back because he doesn't want to impose."

"Paul's a good man, too," Serena said sharply.

The warmth in Giles's heart cooled. Although she was right. Paul was a good man, damn it. And he'd make her a fine husband.

"Indeed he is, sweetheart. And he's desperate to dance with you again, so don't keep him waiting."

Giles had heard enough. He turned and trudged toward the great hall and an evening that promised to be pure torture.

CHAPTER SIX

As soon as Serena returned to the great hall, her sisters commandeered her to play the piano. Belinda and Mary had both taken their turns, and now they joined the dancing as if they were carefree girls, instead of wives and mothers.

Luckily Serena's fingers were so familiar with the quadrilles and cotillions and reels that they didn't betray her distraction. After those disturbing moments in Giles's arms, she welcomed a chance to restore her composure. Moments as disturbing in their way as this afternoon's passionate kisses.

During recent days, she'd felt like a stranger in her own skin. Dancing with Giles, she'd felt as if at last she was in the right place.

Then her mother had interrupted them, and Giles had left her, and she was back to feeling lost and unhappy.

After far too long, she felt enough herself to glance up from her music. Under the boughs of Christmas greenery that decorated the hall, her parents were dancing together, looking like April and May despite over thirty years of marriage. Frederick and the bailiff's pretty daughter made eyes at each other over the punchbowl. Belinda and Mary and their husbands had paused for breath near the refreshments table.

Inevitably her eyes found Giles. He swung the vicar's plump chatterbox of a wife in a wild circle that left her gasping, before he set her under the kissing bough for a peck on the cheek. Since he'd returned to the party, Giles had made a point of partnering the older women and shy girls. She began to suspect that a wide streak of kindness lurked beneath Giles Farraday's worldly ennui.

As she played the end of the reel, Serena smiled at him. When he smiled back, her heart took a disconcerting swoop, and the breath jammed in her throat. Her fingers stumbled, and she blushed at her clumsiness.

"How's my girl tonight?" Paul slid onto the long piano bench beside her.

Usually when Paul singled her out, she was overjoyed. He was such a golden god of a man, any mere mortal felt blessed in his presence. So why tonight did his self-assurance strike a false note? As though the words were right, but the man speaking them was not.

"Am I your girl?" she asked in a cool tone, beginning

a jig and hitting true notes from one end of the keyboard to the other.

"Of course you are." He put his arm around her. "You've always been my girl, and you always will be."

She twisted her shoulders, finding his touch oppressive and his confidence grating. Although nowhere near as grating as the sight of Giles dancing with that hussy Letty Duggan.

"I'm trying to play the piano, Paul." She struggled to hide her irritation.

She must have succeeded. Paul didn't notice. Nor did he take his arm away. "I've hardly seen you since I arrived."

"You know what pandemonium it is when everyone's here for Christmas."

Giles smiled at Letty as if she shone brighter than the stars. Serena struck a sour note. She quickly brought the piece to an end—and felt like cheering when Giles escorted Letty back to her mother and sister.

"I'll take over, if you like," Mary said, bustling across. "You're getting tired."

"You mean I'm playing as if I've got ten thumbs."

"I didn't like to say that." Her sister cast Paul an approving glance. "It's time you two danced. No need to take your duties to extremes, Serena."

"I do like your sister," Paul said with a laugh, as he drew Serena to her feet and onto the floor.

It shouldn't rankle that he hadn't asked her if she

wanted to dance. Nor should it rankle that Giles lingered chatting with the Duggans. When Letty's tinkling laugh rang out, Serena hid a scowl. The local belle wore a dress Serena hadn't seen before. That shade of green didn't suit Letty's complexion. In fact, her color was quite muddy.

"Serena, I'm saying I like your sister," Paul said, and Serena realized she was woolgathering. Which had never happened before in his company.

"She likes you, too," Serena said, lining up for a quadrille. She wondered why she didn't wish it was a waltz. Whirling around the room, clasped tight in Paul's arms, had always been her definition of bliss.

Until she'd kissed Giles...

"I hope the whole family likes me." Taking her hand to walk up the line, he sent her a meaningful look. "Including you."

"You know we all like you," she said lightly, wondering why she wasn't in alt to be his partner.

This Christmas, she spent a cursed lot of time wondering, and she didn't enjoy it one bit.

"But do you like me in particular?" His tone indicated that there could only be one answer to that question.

"Stop fishing for compliments, Paul."

She carried away the memory of his astonished expression, as they peeled apart and worked their way down the line of dancers. By the time they came back to one another, she'd had time to feel ashamed of her grumpiness—and to note that Giles was still talking to Letty Duggan.

"I'm sorry." She strove to come up with a reason for her sharpness. Apart from the fact that she'd obviously lost her mind.

"Don't apologize." Paul smiled with the effortless charm so essential to him. "I deserved a set-down. This is neither the time nor place for the discussion I want to have."

Oh, dear. His graciousness made her feel small and mean. As small and mean as she felt for wanting to rip every rich red hair from Letty's lovely head.

"Let's just enjoy the evening." She hoped Paul didn't hear the desperate note underlying her suggestion.

"Excellent plan," he said easily. "But did you hear what I said?"

She tore her gaze from Giles, who appeared far too cheerful for a brooding loner, devil take him. "You apologized when you didn't have to. I'm acting like a witch."

"Never."

"You're too kind," she said, with her first real smile since he'd joined her on the piano stool.

Paul could be a little smug—a boy coddled by his late parents and generally lauded as a paragon of looks and behavior would hardly grow up to be anything else. But he had a good heart. He wasn't spiteful, and he didn't bear grudges. Even when her childish adoration had become an embarrassment to his adolescent self, he'd remained carelessly kind.

His uncharacteristic seriousness persisted. "I have something important to say to you, Serena. I hope after Christmas, you'll have time and attention to give me a hearing."

Her step faltered, and her stomach dropped about a mile. Not with excitement. "Paul…"

She couldn't mistake his meaning. After years of wanting Paul Garside to notice her, her prayers had been answered. She needed no snares and stratagems after all. Giles had been right. Her quarry was willing to come to her hand.

And the thought made her feel sick.

It was time to have a stern word with herself about constancy.

Then she needed to fall on her knees to the Almighty and offer humble thanks for making all her dreams come true.

But what on earth could she say now? Luckily, Paul's unfailing self-confidence rescued her.

"Cat got your tongue, Serena?" With a tender smile, he touched her cheek, despite the fact that they were surrounded with people. "That doesn't often happen. I feel quite proud of myself."

"I…"

Blast. She sounded a complete nitwit.

His laugh conveyed the affection she'd never doubted. "As I said, this isn't the right time. But wear a pretty dress on Boxing Day and don't stray far from that impressive kissing bough. I have plans for it—and for you."

Before she could dredge up some response, it was their turn to separate again. Thank heaven for the dance's complicated steps.

The moment she left Paul's side, Serena sucked in a deep breath, but nothing shifted the stubborn lump of dread lodged in her chest.

CHAPTER SEVEN

Giles heard Serena's quick step as he waited in the stable yard, holding the saddled horses. With the late winter sunrise, it was still dark, so the rendezvous held a delightfully clandestine air.

"Giles, you're ready for me."

For the life of him, he couldn't tell whether she was pleased to see him or not, as she walked into the circle of light the lantern cast from above the stable doors. "It seemed unfair to disturb the grooms."

Although a groom had poked his head out from the rooms upstairs to check that nobody was stealing Sir George's fine bloodstock at this unearthly hour. When he saw Giles, who had hung around the Talbot stables since boyhood, he'd grunted a greeting and shuffled back to bed.

"Unfair, not to mention indiscreet." They spoke in whispers, heightening the conspiratorial atmosphere. It was deathly cold, and their breath formed clouds before their mouths.

"Well, yes." This time he couldn't mistake Serena's sour tone. As he led her horse forward, he cast her a puzzled glance. His horse was well trained enough to stand waiting. "Would you rather we didn't go?"

She sighed. "I keep forgetting that you're a rake, and intrigues like this are second nature to you."

He frowned. "You asked for my help because I'm a rake."

"That's true. It's unjust to criticize your worldliness when I'm taking advantage of it."

"Quite so." He caught her around the waist, surprising a gasp out of her.

"What are you doing?"

"Good Lord, you're skittish in the mornings." Under his hands, she was as taut as a violin string. "I'm going to toss you up into the saddle. Or would you rather use the mounting block?" His voice lowered. "If you don't want me to touch you, you've dragged me out of bed under false pretenses, which is dashed unsporting on such a cold morning."

She sidled away. "Shh."

"We've often ridden together. And our early start won't be a secret, once the grooms see both horses are gone."

"I know." In the flickering lamplight, her expression was difficult to read. "But we've never ridden alone. And we've never gone riding for the purpose of kisses."

Giles smiled. He liked the sound of that. He'd worried that her jumpiness meant she'd changed her mind. "They can't read your thoughts, Serena."

"Which is a blessing," she said fervently.

Damn, that sounded even better.

When she'd kissed him, he'd had a hard time remembering that she used him as a conduit to Paul. But last night in the library, he'd swear that her attention had belonged to him. At least for part of the time.

Then she'd spent the rest of the night smiling at Garside as if the sun shone out of his arse.

"So you want to do this?"

"Yes," she said. "Faint heart never won fair baronet."

Actually from what Giles had seen last night, Serena could stick Paul's head over her mantelpiece as a trophy, he was so bloody won.

"Then on we go." Trying to sound as if he didn't resent her devotion to Paul, he lifted her onto the black mare.

He mounted his gray gelding, and they rode out of the yard together. Serena was a fine horsewoman, and the strengthening light allowed him to admire the fit of the forest green riding habit trimmed with black frogging.

"In that get-up, you're ready to launch a military campaign."

Beneath the curling brim of her stylish black hat with its jaunty green scarf, she looked fresh and lovely.

The cold added an enchanting glow to her cheeks, and her eyes sparkled with excitement.

Anticipation made his heart leap. Was she excited because she looked forward to his kisses?

"Is there a compliment hidden somewhere there?"

"You're getting above yourself, Miss Talbot."

She laughed. "I'll tell myself there was."

He took the path through the woods behind the house. He knew the Talbot estate better than he knew his own. It hadn't taken him long to choose the location for the next installment in Serena's sensual education.

"I can guess where you're taking me," she said, over the crunch of hooves on the carpet of dead leaves.

"I'm sure you can."

"I'm glad we're not staying outside. It's such a cold day."

The rising sun tinged the stark winter landscape with gold but little warmth. "Don't worry, my pretty little miss." The smile he gave her was full of exaggerated lust. "I'll soon warm you up."

"Perhaps I'll be the one to warm you up," she retorted.

As if one glance from her wasn't enough to make him burn. This morning with kisses in the offing, his blood pumped with barely controlled impatience. But still he must play the game, for fear his urgency might terrify her into running away. "Reckless promises, Miss Talbot."

He couldn't mistake the devilry in her eyes. "Not as reckless as I intend to be, my dear Lord Hallam." She set her heels to her horse, and the mare broke into a canter.

Giles gave a short laugh, as the heat inside him blazed high to defy the icy morning. He set off after Serena, and soon they were galloping through the trees. They were both breathless when she drew rein at a rustic Greek temple beside the silvery gray lake.

She leaned down to pat her horse. "I guessed right?"

"You did indeed. It will be more private than the church."

"Definitely in its favor." She slid to the ground before he could dismount and help her. More was the pity. "You know, I almost had kittens when Paul tried the door."

"Kittens? That's nothing. Mine were elephants and rhinos." He jumped down and crossed to tie his horse to the railing beside the pretty little structure with its Corinthian columns and glass domed roof.

"One would never guess." Serena followed, leading her mare. "You handled him so cleverly."

Giles wasn't so sure that Paul believed in his newfound interest in funerary monuments. "At least I kept you out of harm's way."

"Thank you."

"You know, you're a quick learner." He turned to her. "If you kiss old Paul the way you kissed me, he'll be putty in your hands. You can start choosing your bridesmaids."

Flicking her crop against her gloved palm, she studied him. "Are you trying to avoid another lesson?"

No, he was trying to do the right thing. However belated. However halfhearted. "No. But I'm not sure Paul would see that all this is purely for his benefit."

Dear God, shut the hell up. He'd spent nearly twenty years wanting to kiss Serena Talbot. Yesterday she'd taken him as close to heaven as he was likely to get. But he couldn't bear to think she might regret what they did.

"My conscience is clear." She paused. "It would be different if Paul and I had reached an understanding. Then I'd be betraying a promise. But as things are, I'm as free to kiss you as Paul."

Giles frowned. There was some flaw in her reasoning. But every time she said the word "kiss," she chipped away at his capacity for rational thought.

"You're thinking too much, Giles." She took his gloved hand. "It's a bad habit."

By God, it was. Here he was alone with Serena, and he wasted time worrying about his rival.

He led her up the shallow steps into the temple. The building was open to the elements, and it was as cold inside as out. Perfect for a warm summer day. Perishing a few days before Christmas.

She released his hand. "I'm willing to proceed with our lessons. Are you?"

"I'm a man, my dear." He swept off his hat and tossed it toward the stone bench encircling the octagonal room. He missed. Who cared? "I'm always ready to kiss a pretty girl."

"Does that include Letty?"

He frowned. His brain really was slow today. "What in Hades has Miss Duggan to do with anything?"

The winter dawn flooded the space with pallid light, revealing his beloved with breathtaking clarity. The pink in Serena's cheeks deepened, as she took off her hat and set it and her crop on the black and white tiles. "You seemed to like her last night."

"She's a nice girl, and a treat for the eye." He frowned, still puzzled by the conversation's turn, before he caught a flash of chagrin in Serena's bright silver gaze.

By God, she was jealous. Of Giles Farraday.

Perhaps his case wasn't as hopeless as he thought.

Renewed optimism made him smile down at her with untrammeled delight. He'd chosen this devious course with the frail hope of diverting her interest in Paul. Jealousy was an encouraging sign. Very encouraging indeed.

"Then perhaps you should kiss her instead," Serena said sharply, putting the lie to her words by stripping off her gloves and tossing them down with visible vexation.

Giles's first impulse was to fling himself at her feet and declare that only one woman held his heart. But he hadn't wasted his years in London, and he knew better than to discard the advantages this unexpected development brought.

With a languor designed to taunt, he removed his own gloves and pushed them into his pocket. "She hasn't asked for my kisses."

"I'm sure she will," she sniped.

"What a delightful prospect," Giles drawled. "But something for future consideration. At present, you're here, and Miss Duggan isn't."

She didn't look pleased. Which pleased him. Right now, Paul held no place in her thoughts. "You really are a rake."

He let his smile widen, become predatory, as he took her hand and drew her behind one of the square pillars framing the open doorway. Nowhere in the airy temple was private, but this provided some cover, and gave him a view of the clearing around the temple. Not that anyone was likely to intrude at this hour on a freezing morning.

He let her go. "Shall we begin?"

"I feel a little awkward." She bit her lip in a way that made him want to kiss her until she forgot any nonsense about Letty Duggan. Hell, until she forgot the rest of the world. And she admitted that the only man she wanted was Giles Farraday.

"No need." Maintaining his louche manner, he leaned back against the pillar and folded his arms. Yesterday a careless air had coaxed her into surrender.

Would it work again today? "You did very well. For a beginner."

"Giles, must you tease?"

Oh, no, she started to take his measure.

"It establishes the right tone in the classroom." When he set his hands on her waist, she didn't jump. More progress. He fumbled in his pocket. "And I've brought the necessary equipment."

"Giles!" she gasped, looking shocked and intrigued at the same time. "For shame."

A low laugh escaped. "Serena, I'm appalled. A sweet young miss shouldn't understand that joke."

She rolled her eyes. "As if I wouldn't understand, after all those holidays with you and Paul and Frederick. For pity's sake, you three spent every minute between the ages of eleven and sixteen sniggering— and drooling over the milkmaids."

"I'm sure we were charming."

She laughed. "I'm sure you weren't. But you've all improved since, thank goodness."

"Well, that's something." He drew his hand from his pocket and opened it to reveal what lay on his palm. "And you mistake me. This is what I meant."

"Where did you get that?"

"The kissing bough at the manor. I didn't want to risk a refusal."

"As if I'd refuse." She shot him an unimpressed glance. "I invited you, remember?"

He lifted the mistletoe over her ruffled blond head

and brushed a light kiss over her lips. The ride and the removal of her hat had made a delightful mess of this morning's severe chignon. He loved to see her like this, sweet and ardent and disheveled.

"Time to see what you remember from yesterday's lessons." He dropped the sprig and lashed his arms around her, drawing her up for a kiss that wasn't light at all.

CHAPTER EIGHT

*S*erena sank into the sultry darkness of Giles's kiss. With an incoherent murmur of welcome, she opened to his heated exploration. The sweep of his tongue inside her mouth engulfed her in pleasure.

And desire.

Because today, she felt more than surprise and curiosity. Today she craved.

Instinctively she sucked on his tongue, drawing him deeper into her mouth. With a growl of approval, he bundled her closer to his powerful body.

How had she missed what an impressive figure of a man Giles was? At Torver, he tended to allow Paul and Frederick to hold the limelight. But as her feverish hands stroked his shoulders and back, she couldn't mistake the hard, vital muscle under her palms.

How fascinating he turned out to be. The line of his

jaw was hard and adamant, betraying a strength she'd never troubled to notice. His skin was smooth—she guessed he'd shaved before coming downstairs—but gave an intriguing hint of his beard.

Sinful curiosity ate at her. What other marvels lay beneath his elegant dark blue coat and soft white shirt?

When she twined her arms around his neck and her breasts met his chest, the sensation turned her knees to wet string. Yesterday's kiss had been astonishing, a revelation. Today's promised to change her forever. This heady delight was worth all the risk in the world.

She flicked her tongue over his in a silent plea for more passion. Although a whisper at the back of her mind warned her that she verged perilously close to folly.

But folly was so warm and bright and beckoning. How could she say no?

The kiss broke through into wildness. Giles's touch turned demanding, and his lips plundered hers, giving no quarter to her innocence. She thrilled to every wanton, blazing caress. Dark temptation lured her to the edge of yielding everything, and she was helpless to resist.

His hands touched her body, stroking her sides and her back, trailing sizzling heat down her hips. A forbidden moment when he cupped the curve of her backside. Then for an incandescent instant, his hand settled on her breast and squeezed. Excitement hot as a naked flame zigzagged through her.

With a guttural groan that resonated in her bones, Giles wrenched his hands from her. "For God's sake, Serena, forgive me."

She whimpered in protest as he staggered back, panting. It was wrong, she knew it was wrong. But she'd give up her hope of heaven to have that large male hand touch her breast again.

Serena's gaze dropped. She blushed and looked up in a hurry. His breeches did little to hide his excitement. That kiss had tested his control, as well as hers.

She gulped in a ragged breath, hoping it would calm her rioting pulse. It didn't.

Her chastity had never been an onerous burden. She'd known that one day she'd surrender her virginity to Paul Garside in the sanctified space of a marriage bed. Stupidly, she'd never much considered the actual act.

Now, staring into Giles Farraday's glittering dark eyes, she realized that despite her girlish adoration, she'd never hungered for Paul. But dear Lord above, how she hungered for Giles. For his kisses. For his teasing which made her feel they shared a joke nobody else got. For, heaven forgive her, lying beside him with no barriers between them, not even clothing. For that long, powerful body to pound into her.

Giles sucked in an audible, shuddering breath. Heavy eyelids lowered over his eyes, the thick, black eyelashes sweeping down. These details of his appearance enthralled her. This Christmas, she'd noticed so many small beauties that once she'd been blind to.

Paul was like the sun, his light eclipsing all other satellites. Except Serena now admitted that Giles Farraday was nobody's satellite. His attractions were subtle, almost self-effacing—and all the more powerful for that.

Her wondering gaze traced his face. The raw bone structure, the expressive lips, the uneven line of his nose that conveyed more character than any perfect profile could. The thick eyebrows that expressed a universe of reaction with the smallest twitch. The dark eyes that saw so much.

Too much.

Before she could censor herself, she spoke. "You know, I meant it last night—you really are handsome. No wonder the London ladies are mad for you."

His smile was lopsided. "I doubt they want me for my pretty face."

"Then what..." Her voice faded, and heat prickled her cheeks.

With a grunt of laughter, he took her hand and drew her toward the bench. "That answer's beyond the scope of this instruction. After all, I don't want to end up facing either Paul or Frederick down the barrel of a dueling pistol."

Something unhappy crossed his face as they sat, although he sounded just as he always did. Sardonic. Amused. Detached.

Giles hadn't kissed her with detachment. However inexperienced she was, she knew that. Although perhaps she should arrange for him to kiss her until Twelfth Night, just to make sure.

The droll fancy withered as she recalled that Paul intended to propose on Boxing Day.

That prospect really shouldn't make her heart sink.

She'd marry Paul Garside, and Giles would go on to share his secrets—and his kisses—with some other lucky girl. It appalled her quite how much she wanted to rip out that unknown female's hair by the roots. And she'd like to do the same to all his London ladies, too.

"Stop talking." Her hand tightened on his, and she turned toward him. "I came here to learn how to kiss."

Serena couldn't blame him for looking startled. She sounded close to losing her temper. Whereas instead, she was close to losing her mind.

"You don't need more lessons. You graduated with honors."

Hurt stabbed her. While this was a game for him—and supposedly for her—she hadn't expected him to tire of her so quickly. "Don't you want to kiss me again?"

With a hunted expression, he ran one elegant hand through his thick, dark hair, leaving it beguilingly disheveled. "It wouldn't be wise."

"We've only just arrived." For pity's sake, could she sound any more like a whiney child, denied a treat? "You can't send me away yet."

"Serena…" He paused. "Who the devil decided to call you Serena? I can't think of a less appropriate name."

"My father did. Don't change the subject. Why are you being difficult?"

His expression turned austere. "I don't trust myself to kiss you again."

Relief flooded her. "So you do want to kiss me?"

"Hell, Serena." He surged to his feet and retreated, staring at her as if she might bite him. With a soft crunch, his heel crushed the sprig of mistletoe. "You don't understand."

She remained on the bench, watching him. "So make me understand."

"Devil take you, this isn't a conversation a man has with a close friend's sister."

She worked to keep her voice steady and said what she knew in her heart to be true. "You want me."

"You're a pretty girl. Nothing could be more natural."

Why did she feel like she wasn't getting the whole story? "Nothing."

Her fingers itched to order his hair, to smooth the lines of discontent marking his face. But she stayed where she was, struggling to make sense of his reluctance. He'd set off from the stables, intending to kiss her. Then he'd kissed her. Now it seemed he'd give her no more kisses.

Serena sat up straight and summoned all her

courage. "I see that kissing isn't enough for you. For a sophisticated man, it's all too schoolboy and schoolgirl."

"Don't talk rot." His hunted expression intensified. "I don't even know why you want me to chase you, when you're so set on marrying Paul. He's the one you should meet secretly. He's the one you should drive mad with kisses."

"I told you why."

He turned away to stare out at the lake. Ruler-straight shoulders betrayed bristling tension. "You wanted to test your wiles on a man who doesn't matter, before you use them on the man you want."

Humiliation coiled in her belly as her hands gripped the edge of the bench. "That sounds horribly shabby." When he didn't respond, she burst out, "If kissing me offends your high standards, why on earth did you agree in the first place?"

Without looking at her, he set his hands against the window frame. "Serena, are you going to marry Paul?"

The coiling in her stomach turned out to be snakes with fangs. "He hasn't asked me."

"He will."

"You don't know that."

"Yes, I do. He told me."

Of course he had. For heaven's sake, Paul had all but told her. If she'd offered one word of encouragement last night, he'd have whisked her off somewhere private and proposed. "I've wanted to marry Paul all my life."

Giles finally faced her. He looked stern, and years older than twenty-six. "In that case, it's wrong to kiss me."

She flinched from that stark assessment. "You knew all this when we started."

"Yes, well, it turns out that I have more of a conscience than I knew." His smile was bitter. "Paul's a friend, and you're an innocent, and all three of us deserve better than this."

Rising on trembling legs, she shot Giles a glare of genuine dislike. While inside, razors cut her to ribbons. "So that's it?"

He gestured an apology. "I'm afraid it is."

"That's...cruel."

He shook his head. "No, it's the only thing I can do."

She resisted the urge to stamp her foot. "You're so blasted stubborn."

Something that looked like sorrow flashed in his eyes. But it vanished before she could be sure. "I expect you hate me now."

Serena was angry and piqued and cringing with mortification. But the truth was that when she examined her emotions, she didn't hate him. What she mainly felt was piercing regret that his exquisite kisses were out of bounds. Which was lunatic when she meant to accept Paul's proposal on Boxing Day.

Her silence made him sigh. "I hope you'll forgive me one day."

"For kissing me?" she asked through lips as stiff as wood. "Or for giving me my marching orders?"

Faint humor eased his expression. "Both."

With a sharp click of her heels on tile, she crossed to collect her belongings. The cold in the summerhouse was biting. Strange she only noticed now.

"I'm glad you find this funny." With short, sharp movements, she put on her hat and gloves and turned toward the door with a defiant swing of her hips. "I'd hate to think educating a clumsy beginner provided no entertainment."

"Serena…" He stepped forward, but she raised her crop to gesture him back.

In a distant corner of her mind, she knew he was right to question their actions. But that didn't take the sting away. Or make her any more prepared to be fair to him.

His kisses had flung her into a dazzling new world. Now without warning, he hurled her back onto the sharp rocks of harsh reality. "My thanks for deigning to show me what I've been missing, Lord Hallam."

"Lord Hallam?" Those expressive brows slanted in not entirely convincing mockery. "You really are angry with me."

She didn't smile. "You won't tease me back into charity with you, Giles."

"At least I teased you back into calling me Giles.

Can't we just admit we both made a mistake and pretend it never happened?" With an attempt at his old nonchalance, he leaned one shoulder against the pillar.

The last few days had taught her more about Giles Farraday than the previous eighteen years. He might want her to believe he laughed off this dismissal, but she didn't believe him. She also knew that he'd let stampeding elephants trample him before he explained himself further.

She nodded coldly in his direction. "You know, I'm not sure we can."

Serena caught his shocked dismay, as she turned toward the door and marched out. Anger, and hurt, and a sexual frustration she'd never felt before Giles had kissed her roiled in her stomach. Tears she was too proud to shed stung her eyes.

How dare that oaf Giles Farraday make her cry?

Gracelessly she scrambled into the saddle. As she wheeled the horse around, Giles appeared at the top of the steps. At least he was smart enough not to offer to help her mount. The touch of those deft hands would be unbearable. If only because it provided a painful reminder of the pleasures he denied her.

She waited for him to speak. Apologize again. Or accuse her of overreacting. Or least likely, but most longed for, call her inside for more kisses. Because the awful truth was that even now, if he invited her back into his arms, she'd go. Pride be damned.

But he continued to watch her with an unwavering regard. And this time, he didn't pretend to indifference.

For an intense interval, their eyes met, and she wondered how she could ever have overlooked him. He was the most striking man she'd ever met.

Her horse stamped in impatience at the delay, but Serena held the mare and studied Giles, imprinting his image on her mind forever. The tall, lean body. The rumpled black hair. The quirky, intelligent face that lately seemed so much more appealing than mere good looks.

Something strong and dark rushed through her, something that wasn't a game at all.

With an abrupt gesture, she set her heels to her horse so the mare bounded into a gallop. But as she dashed through the trees, nothing could erase the memory of Giles standing, proud and solitary, in that frame of white marble.

Solitary. And heartbreakingly lonely.

CHAPTER NINE

Giles leaned back in the leather chair in front of the library fire, stretched his legs toward the grate, and stared unseeingly at the plaster flowers and garlands twining across the ceiling. An empty glass dangled from his fingers. He'd hoped brandy might ease the ache in his loins—and the sharper ache in his heart.

Chance would be a fine thing. All the liquor in the world couldn't wash away his hopeless longing.

It was late, and he was alone. Again. After dinner, the guests had spread through the house. The children, allowed to stay downstairs because tomorrow was Christmas Eve, and their parents played games in the drawing room. The older guests sat at cards in the morning room. Frederick and Paul had invited Giles to play billiards, but he'd declined. When a man said farewell to a dream, he was allowed an evening to wallow in despair before facing up to a desolate future.

Unrequited love was the very devil, and a conscience was nothing but a damned inconvenience. The worst of it was that now he knew the magic of Serena's kiss, his torment bit deeper than ever.

He was well repaid for his nasty little plot to wreck Paul's plans.

What a bloody fool he was. Of course he hadn't won. Paul and Serena were made for each other. Destined from birth to marry. Much as he hated to admit it, they'd be happy. God rot it. Watching Paul and Serena make sheeps' eyes at one another at tonight's dinner, hearing her laugh at his jokes, imagining the whole world celebrating their engagement, made Giles want to shoot himself.

Paul's company chafed like sandpaper, although he'd been Giles's best friend since they'd started at Eton. Paul had fought beside him when the school bullies had decided to put that swarthy, fatherless oddity, Lord Hallam, in his place. More recently, Paul had explored London's pleasures with him.

Now Giles consigned handsome, charming, good-natured Paul Garside, the companion to whom he owed so much, to the deepest pit in Hades.

He sighed heavily and thought without interest about refilling his glass. And about leaving. There was nothing to be gained from staying in Dorset. He should go back to London.

Except there he might encounter the happy couple.

His estates in Devon? No, still within reach.

Perhaps he should sail for India. With luck, a hungry tiger might put him out of his misery.

Because nothing but annihilation would stop him wanting Serena. Even then, he'd probably come back and haunt her.

When he'd set out to stymie his friend's wedding, he'd intended little more than a flirtation to show Serena that life didn't begin and end with Paul bloody Garside. But her kisses were as addictive as opium, and they turned a man's brain to porridge. At the church, the possibility of discovery had kept a rein on his desires. In the isolated summerhouse, he'd rapidly reached a point where kisses weren't enough.

And they had to be.

Giles couldn't deflower Frederick's sister while he was a guest in the Talbot house. But her dangerous willingness to follow his lead had enticed him to the verge of the unforgivable.

He'd misjudged the powerful effect of his beloved's nearness. Keeping his hands to himself had been simple when Serena treated him as a vague acquaintance. When he held her in his arms, control became impossible. He'd stepped away, the only thing he could do to preserve honor. His and hers.

And incurred not gratitude, but chastisement for his efforts.

He stared into the fire, recalling that nasty quarrel.

And the pain shining in her gray eyes, pain that all the pique in the world couldn't conceal.

Like an echo of last night, the door clicked shut behind him.

God give him strength. If Serena sought him out again, he wouldn't be responsible for his actions. Although given the way she'd refused to look at him all night, he couldn't imagine she wanted his company.

No, in sending her away, he'd fatally wounded her pride. Regret added its doleful note to the dismal music playing in his soul. He'd done the right thing, but he could have been gentler.

He'd been so near to using her innocent response as an invitation to take things further, that he hadn't been in command of himself. She'd had a lucky escape this morning. Although she'd never thank him for it.

When the intruder didn't speak, Giles angled his head around the chair's high back.

His heart plummeted. It wasn't Serena.

It was worse.

Wearing a hard expression Giles had never seen before, Paul stood four-square in the center of the library. There was no trace of the lighthearted comrade who had shared so many escapades. "I should have known. You always sneak away to a library when things get too hot in the real world."

"Just wanted a minute's peace, old chap. We confirmed bachelors sometimes find family life a bit much."

Paul didn't smile. Which was odd. Giles had long ago decided that Paul could smile through a hurricane.

Foreboding stirred. A foreboding the next words confirmed.

"And of course you're hoping this brooding act will trick Serena into looking for you."

Slowly Giles rose. "I haven't spoken to Serena all night."

"At least you don't insult me by pretending to misunderstand."

Giles sighed and turned toward the sideboard. "Would you like a drink?"

"No."

"She doesn't want me." Giles poured another brandy. He had a grim inkling he might need it. "She wants you."

"That's right."

Moving deliberately, pretending that a row with his best friend wasn't imminent, he turned. "You know, old pal, that overweening confidence might get you into trouble."

"You'd like to think so."

Actually Giles offered the advice without self-interest. Or not much. He'd never had a chance with Serena. Even less after today.

He shrugged. "Just warning you."

Paul stepped closer, his shoulders straight and his hands forming fists at his sides. "And I'm warning you

—stay away from the woman I intend to marry, or bloody well take the consequences."

Despite the confrontation's seriousness, Giles gave a derisive snort. "You might have been able to beat me in a physical contest when we were boys, Garside. But I wouldn't be too sure that's the case now."

Anger narrowed Paul's eyes. "You're proving a pest, Hallam. I saw you go riding with Serena this morning, and I'll wager you chased her into the church the day before. Nobody in their right mind would believe that you've turned into a musty, fusty antiquarian. Credit me with some intelligence."

Unfortunately, he did. People might see the large, benevolent baronet, and mistake his easygoing nature for stupidity. Giles had never made that error.

Despite wisdom counseling retreat, he taunted his rival. "How do you explain her sudden interest in my company?"

"That's simple. She's trying to raise the stakes before she says yes to marrying me. No woman likes to be won too easily. In her opinion, a little jealousy will do me good."

The hell of it was that Paul was right.

"Serena is as pure as the day we met," Giles said curtly. Paul didn't need to know that was thanks to Giles dredging up some barely maintained strength of character.

"Of course she is." Paul brushed the statement aside.

"She knows as well as I do that we're meant to be together."

"So why are you worried?" Giles stifled the unworthy impulse to tell Paul how Serena had begged for his kisses.

But then she'd made it clear that Paul Garside was her choice. Not much of a triumph for Giles, after all.

"I'm not worried. I just don't like to see you making a fool of yourself."

"So kind," Giles said drily.

"You've always had an eye for her. I can't blame you. She's a pretty girl." Paul sounded a little more conciliatory. For a second there, Giles had worried that his best friend meant to thump him. Or worse, shoot him at dawn.

That would spoil everyone's Christmas.

"Nothing's set in stone," Giles said, risking a return of his friend's belligerence.

But Paul's temper had subsided, and he was again his affable, supremely assured self. "The engagement has been planned since she was in the cradle."

"These last years in London, you haven't behaved like an engaged man."

Paul's laugh was short. "A man has a right to enjoy his freedom. None of those women meant anything. I intend to be a faithful husband. So if you're hoping to sniff around a betrayed wife, you're wasting your time. Serena will have no cause to complain of my straying."

Giles bit back his own temper. Something inside

him, probably the sour residue of failure, screamed that this practical marriage left Serena shortchanged. Paul was fond of Serena—might actually love her. If he did, he wouldn't confess that to a friend. Even less to a rival.

"She deserves to be happy."

"She will be. With me. So I suggest from now on, you avoid Serena's company."

Not appreciating the position Paul placed him in, that of naughty little boy forcing himself in where he wasn't wanted, Giles tossed back his brandy. "Given we're sharing a house, that might be a problem."

Paul regarded him steadily. "You're a clever sod. You'll work something out." He paused. "And you should make plans to leave on Boxing Day."

Giles slammed his glass down on the sideboard. "You have no right to throw me out of another man's house."

"Only trying to save you from having to put on a polite face when we announce our engagement." He shot Giles a hostile look under his golden eyebrows. "And don't be in a hurry to visit us, once we're married. I'm sure you'll have better things to do."

Humiliation churned in Giles's belly. He couldn't blame Paul for protecting his interests. But it was no fun being on the receiving end of the reprimand. "Is that what Serena wants?"

He saw Paul consider, then dismiss a lie. "I thought we should have a private word first. She's fond of you, in her way. I don't want her feeling sorry for you."

Bravo, Garside. Giles barely hid a wince, although his hand clenched against the sideboard. Fondness and pity. How cleverly Paul damned Giles's futile hopes.

"Have you finished?" he asked through tight lips.

Paul's smile was superior. "No hard feelings, my friend." He cast a derisive glance at his empty glass. "Have another drink, and accept the best man won."

He moved forward and clapped Giles on the shoulder. Giles was hard put not to strike that large, capable hand away.

Only once Paul had gone did he release a shuddering breath. His friend must be more than a little concerned, if he brought himself to warn Giles off in such terms.

Had Giles felt generous, he could have told Paul that Serena intended to accept his proposal.

Giles, however, wasn't feeling generous.

CHAPTER TEN

After their quarrel in the summerhouse, Giles stayed out of Serena's way. His skill at managing this impressed her. After all, despite the crowd, they were under one roof, and the weather had taken a turn for the worse, so everyone was confined indoors.

But he seemed to have an uncanny ability to know when she approached. She'd walk into a room, lured by the deep rumble of his voice. Yet Giles would prove absent. The funny little skip in her pulse would subside to a disappointed chug.

She saw him at meals, and he joined the other guests for the midnight Christmas service and all the games and festivities today. Now Christmas Day drew toward evening, the children had retired exhausted to the nursery, and her sisters had started playing silly, giggly games under the kissing bough.

Serena felt like the specter at the feast. This year, seasonal cheer galled. She wished she was anywhere but here with her happy, laughing, loving family. And hated herself for her sourness.

After all, she had nothing to complain about. She'd wanted Paul to make his intentions clear this Christmas, and he'd spent all day pursuing her. Until she was ready to scream.

She only had a moment to herself now, standing beside the roaring fire, because Mary had dragged Paul under the mistletoe and was making him kiss every female in the house, from eighty-year-old Great-Aunt Agatha down to Cousin Jane, who at fourteen was enjoying her first grown-up celebrations. Her blushing elation as handsome Sir Paul Garside brushed his lips over her cheek pierced Serena's grumpiness and reminded her of the first time Paul had kissed her, just so chastely, when she was fourteen. It had been the greatest thrill of her young life and only confirmed her determination to become his wife one day.

She tried to remind herself that her dreams had always focused on Paul. But inevitably her gaze slid away, to where Giles stood with Frederick, observing the hilarity with a sardonic eye.

Except after the last few days, she saw beneath that elegant detachment to the feelings he hid so well. Across the crowded hall—naturally he'd chosen a position as far from her as he could devise without leaving the room—she sensed his deep unhappiness. Her stupid heart cramped with painful longing to ease his isolation.

But she was the last person he'd turn to for comfort. His disdain couldn't be clearer. Serena had had plenty of time to work out what sparked his behavior in the summerhouse. Because she'd welcomed his kisses, he now thought she was a shameless hussy, which didn't seem fair when he'd kissed her just as eagerly.

Men had such bizarre notions.

Out of the corner of her eye, she saw Paul whisper something to Mary. So it was no surprise when her sister moved purposefully toward Serena.

"Stop moping over here," she said. "It's time to kiss your beau."

Serena bit back an instinctive protest. Because Paul was her beau. Tomorrow he'd propose, and he'd be more than her beau, he'd become her betrothed. She felt trapped in a tide that she was powerless to stop.

Just as she was powerless to stop her sister from hauling her under the kissing bough.

"Mary—"

"You can enjoy something more private later." Her sister's arch expression made Serena want to slap her into next week. "But keep it light now."

"At last!" At Serena's approach, Paul opened his arms wide, and his smile made her feel like a Christmas pudding presented to a starving man. "I thought you'd hover over there, playing hard to get, until Easter."

"I wasn't—" She gasped as Mary shoved her hard in

the back. Losing her footing, she crashed into Paul. With unrestrained enthusiasm, his arms closed around her.

All her dreams were coming true. And she hated it.

She stiffened and tried to push free, but he was too strong. It seemed she must grin and bear what was to come. She snatched a shuddering breath, heavy with Paul's scent: bay rum, horses, and healthy, virile male. It was a nice smell. It shouldn't seem completely wrong.

Gritting her teeth and wanting to throttle her sister, she rose on her toes and skimmed her lips across his cheek. The contact was over in an instant, and Serena prepared to retreat.

"You can do better than that," Mary scoffed.

Serena turned her head and saw that everyone was watching. She caught Giles's unreadable dark gaze before he glanced away. Shame heated her cheeks. How he must despise her for rushing from his kisses to Paul's.

"No need to be shy, sweetheart," Paul murmured, his hold on her waist firming. "Everybody knows we have an understanding."

Another glance confirmed that if she didn't count Giles, their audience radiated approval.

She'd devoted years to dreaming of Paul's kisses. Perhaps he was right about her being shy. His kiss might shatter her odd, contrary mood, like a prince breaking a wicked spell in a fairytale.

She raised her head and pursed her lips, saying a frantic prayer for magic. Paul's lips descended. The kiss was innocent—although until a few days ago, she wouldn't have recognized that—and tinged with tenderness.

Serena stood unmoved.

After what felt like an eon, Paul withdrew to regard her with a satisfaction that seemed unwarranted. Or perhaps Giles's kisses had turned her into a hopeless wanton, capable of responding only to voracious passion.

For one blind, reckless moment, she considered tugging Paul closer and insisting on something more carnal. Her hand curled in his shirt.

Then everyone around them burst into applause, and she realized now was neither the time nor the place. Paul laughed and leaned forward to kiss her cheek, whispering for her ears alone, "The first of many delightful kisses to come, I hope."

Before she could summon an answer—and what could she say?—he stepped away with a brief bow, leaving her standing under the kissing bough.

"Serena's in place. Does anyone else want to kiss her?" Mary asked.

Before she could escape, her brother, her brothers-in-law, her uncles, her cousins, and her father lined up. Most made do with a peck on the cheek, although Charles, her oldest cousin, tried to kiss her lips. As he grabbed her waist and his flushed face loomed closer, she strained away. The alcohol on his breath made her dizzy.

"Charles, you're foxed."

"Dash it, Serena, you're awfully pretty—and it's Christmas after all."

"And you've been celebrating too hard," she snapped.

"If you refuse to kiss me, you won't get married next year," he said snidely.

Right now, that seemed a blessing. She gave Charles a brief kiss on the cheek and shoved him away.

"Careful," he grunted, stumbling into the people behind him.

"Grow up, Charles," Giles said firmly. "And stay away from the rum punch. You'll have a devil of a head in the morning, as it is."

"Damn it. Can't a man kick up his heels at Christmas?" Charles grumbled, but once he'd found his feet, he shambled off without causing any more trouble.

Serena's gaze settled on Giles, and a deep, tingling warmth rose from her toes to her crown, until she was sure she must glow like a candle.

"Giles…" she murmured, hardly believing he lined up to kiss her. Then she noticed Mary's implacable hand curled around his arm.

"I saw Giles hanging back and couldn't let him escape," Mary said.

Serena glared at her sister. "You're very free with another woman's kisses."

Mary shrugged. "Giles can't be the only gentleman in the house who misses out on a kiss."

"I'm sure he's big enough to ask for his own kisses," she said acidly, before she blushed a painful red. She remembered a time when he'd done just that, and she'd been quick to comply.

"I'd count myself privileged to kiss Serena." His voice was level, but she knew he had to be sarcastic. After all, in the summerhouse, he could have kissed her to his heart's content, and he'd decided he wasn't interested.

"Do your worst," she said, bracing and presenting her cheek.

He seemed to take forever to move. She held her breath until her head swam.

Leaning in, he glanced his lips across her cheek. The contact was over in a second.

Unlike Paul, Giles didn't fling his arms around her or try to kiss her on the lips. For heaven's sake, her brother and father had shown more warmth.

Yet a thousand vivid impressions assailed her and banished everything but his nearness from her mind. The noisy, crowded room faded away, and all she knew was Giles. His height. His delicious scent. The cool touch of his lips on her skin.

She closed her eyes and told herself she had nothing to cry about. Even as a tight ball of tears jammed in her throat.

She was so attuned to Giles that she heard his

breath catch when he shifted away. Her hand rose to draw him back.

Then Serena heard him speak to Mary and realized she was about to make a complete fool of herself. She forced her hand back to her side, opened her eyes, and struggled to act as if nothing had happened.

Because of course it hadn't. A friendly kiss beneath the mistletoe meant nothing. It was just a Christmas game they played every year.

"There, Mary, are you satisfied?" he asked lightly.

Her sister batted her eyelashes, as if Giles was her new flirt, when she'd been happily married for the last six years. "What about me?" She pouted with exaggerated chagrin. "Why should Serena have all the fun?"

"You're a managing wench." Giles gave her sister a proper smile.

Serena had no idea when she'd become such a connoisseur of Giles Farraday's smiles, but all day, he'd done his best to give an appearance of enjoyment he didn't feel. His smile for Mary was wry and fond, and nearly broke Serena's heart. Because once upon a time, he'd smiled at her like that. But no longer. And she couldn't bear that she'd lost him, just as she started to appreciate his qualities.

With her hip, Mary bumped Serena away from the mistletoe. "Managing wenches get all the kisses."

Serena seized the opportunity to scuttle off. Usually she loved having the family together for Christmas. This year, she observed the laughing crowd playing snapdragon, and the group standing around the piano singing carols, and the guests enjoying a good natter with people they rarely saw, and wished every one of them to perdition.

She saw Paul fill two glasses of champagne and turn around, obviously looking for her. *No, no, no. Not now when she felt so shaken and uncertain.*

Putting her head down, she made blindly for the corridor. She could no longer pretend that this Christmas was like every other Christmas.

"Serena? Is something wrong?"

As she bumped into her mother in the doorway, she glanced up frantically. She met gray eyes, so like her own, and battled the urge to pour out all her unhappiness and confusion.

But her mother was busy, hosting this huge house party. Serena couldn't burden someone who already had so much to do. Anyway, what could she say? Nothing made sense to her. She hadn't a hope of explaining these bewildering emotions to anyone else.

"No," she said in a choked voice. She struggled to find a reason for running away as if demons from hell pursued her. Across the room, she saw Paul craning his neck over the crowd. "I...I need something from my room."

She didn't wait for her mother's response. Instead she picked up her skirts and dashed into the blessed quiet of the hallway.

She sucked in a breath close to a sob. If she stayed

so close to the party, Paul would find her, and that suddenly seemed the worst fate possible.

Wildly she looked around for somewhere to hide. If she took refuge in her bedroom, her mother might decide to check on her. Outside was no good. The snow fell in buckets, and an icy wind howled.

Her glance fell on the door to the library. Not even Paul's greatest admirer would call him a bookish man. This was her best bet for avoiding him.

She whisked into the room and whirled to close the door, when she glanced up to see Giles a few steps behind her. With a shuddering gasp, she faltered back as he strode forward and shut them inside. Alone.

Neither spoke a word as he seized her with ruthless hands and swept her into his arms.

CHAPTER ELEVEN

When his mouth slammed down onto Serena's, Giles heard a soft growl of feminine appreciation. She arched into him and clutched at his hair to tug him closer. Her mouth opened hot and greedy under his.

Heat gushed through him, incinerated all thought of her innocence and the danger of coming together like this, so close to discovery. For two days, she'd barely spared him a kind word. While all the time, his frustration and hunger mounted—hell, he'd hungered for her all his life. That polite kiss in full view had been torture. When she left the room, he'd yielded to the overpowering need to speak to her alone.

Except they weren't talking.

Panting, he ripped his lips free of hers. "Serena..." he said, like a drowning man snatching a final breath before he went under for the last time.

Her eyes were stormy, and she pulled his hair to the point of pain. "Don't talk."

She was right. What the devil use was talking?

Giles kissed her again, hard and furious. As if he hated her. He'd been in love for years, yet he'd never realized love could be like this. Like someone struck him with a club over and over again. Like fire devouring him. Sweet and terrible. Painful and fierce.

Serena bit at his lips, stoking his desire with the sting.

"I didn't teach you that," he said roughly.

To his surprise, she responded with a low laugh. "I'm experimenting."

"You'll kill me before you're finished," he groaned.

She rose on her toes to kiss him again. "What a lovely way to die."

Through the steam filling his head, Giles realized that she was as mad for him as he was for her. How astonishing. How magnificent. Her hot mouth, her exploring hands, the incoherent sounds she made, all conspired to annihilate judgment.

He scraped his teeth along her throat, making her shiver. A few tugs, and her hair tumbled down in a slippery mass. He sucked hard at the sensitive place where her neck met her shoulder, until she was shaking and gasping. When his hand shaped her breast, she started with excitement, and her nipple beaded against his palm.

It wasn't enough. He needed to touch her skin.

He dragged her bodice down, some frothy pink concoction cut low across her bosom. As she murmured encouragement, his hand closed around one exposed breast. Warm flesh, silky skin. Arousal shuddered through him, and he thrust his hips forward.

Instead of withdrawing, she angled in and hooked her hand behind his neck. As if he was drunk, he staggered toward the wall opposite the closed door. Serena landed with a bump that jolted the breath from her.

Giles raised his head and caught the blazing excitement in her face. She'd never been more beautiful. His heart gave one huge thump, then another. His love for her was inescapable.

"For pity's sake, don't stop," Serena said in a broken voice he hadn't heard before.

"Never," he vowed, staring down at her breast.

Satiny white skin gleamed in the candlelight. He bent to draw the raspberry nipple between his lips. Her taste set his senses rioting, and he sucked hard, reveling in her cracked cry of pleasure. She sagged against the wall, and his grip on her waist tightened. His tongue and teeth teased her breast, until she was gasping and arching. She was pure flame in his arms, everything he'd dreamed and more.

"That's…wicked," she whispered.

He smiled into her flesh and bit down softly. A delicious shudder rippled through her. Without conscious thought—he operated on animal instinct alone—his hand clenched in her filmy skirts and edged upward. He thirsted to learn the secrets of her body. He thirsted to claim her.

When he raised his head from her breast, she leaned against the wall as if her legs wouldn't support her. Her eyes were closed, and the erratic breath escaped between her parted, swollen lips. The glimpse of straight white teeth behind reddened lips was devastatingly erotic.

He leaned in to nip her lower lip. When she opened, he swept his tongue inside, tasting her hot, wet sweetness. While his seeking hand inched closer to the hot, wet sweetness between her legs.

The scent of her arousal made his head swim. When his fingers brushed her bare thigh, she jerked in response. He deepened the kiss until the blood thundered in his ears.

How he ached to take her. She was trembling and eager, and God knew, he'd been ready for years.

His fingers pushed up the loose drawers, tracing a silky path to bliss. She shifted to give him access. When his fingers slid across soft, intimate curls, he groaned in infinite gratitude. She gave a muffled cry, and her grip on his shoulders tightened.

Giles cupped her mound and dipped his fingers in the liquid honey of her desire. She tipped her head back against the wall and bit her lip to muffle a long moan of surrender. The urge to proceed, to discover and possess all her mysteries, beat around him like a thousand wings.

He was so close, so close...

The door slammed open. As Serena stiffened in his arms, a harsh, angry voice smashed through his idyll.

"You unmitigated bloody bastard!"

Paralyzed with horror, Serena stared over Giles's shoulder to where Paul filled the doorway, large, furious, and undoubtedly suffering hurt feelings.

The vivid heaven of Giles's kiss had flung her a thousand miles from considerations of sin, propriety or scandal. But as she read the stark betrayal on Paul's face, acrid shame set her belly heaving and made her skin break out in goosebumps.

"Stop..." she muttered to Giles, who still crushed her against the wall where, devil curse her recklessness, he'd been within inches of taking her.

Like a doxy at a tavern.

And in her father's house, with her family celebrating Christmas only a room away.

"Serena, it's all right," Giles whispered.

"No, it's not," she grated, pushing him with agitated hands that seconds ago had clutched him to her.

"Get away from her, you sodding mongrel," Paul snarled, barging into the room and crashing into a delicate gilt table, overturning it.

"Keep your blasted voice down." With agonizing slowness, Giles straightened away from her and turned to face Paul. "Do you want every man and his dog in here?"

"You dare to lecture me on decorum?" Paul roared.

Giles stood squarely in front of Serena, blocking her view of Paul. Which right now was a relief, however cowardly that made her.

Self-disgust stabbed her, when she glanced down and noticed her sagging bodice for the first time. She realized Giles was giving her a chance to cover herself. With shaking hands, she tugged her dress into place. More shame, sharp as broken glass.

She couldn't even blame Giles for what had happened. Every step of the way, she'd been his willing partner. Nausea churned in her stomach. She felt cheap and foolish and used.

"Paul..." Clutching her dress to preserve her frail modesty, Serena stepped out from behind Giles.

Unfortunately her intervention made things worse. Paul's attention focused on her rumpled dress, and incandescent anger flooded his face. The bright blue eyes went as black as coal.

"You swine, Hallam. What the hell have you done to her?" He surged forward and slammed his substantial fist into Giles's face.

Serena cried out as Giles staggered under the force of the blow.

"Paul, how could you?" She grabbed for Giles. As he

fought for balance, his arm was as hard as rock under her hand. She braced for him to reciprocate with violence, but he didn't move.

"You had every right to do that," Giles said stiffly, a muscle working in his lean cheek.

Paul regarded him with lacerating contempt. "Fight me, you cur."

"We can't brawl in Lady Talbot's library." Giles moved away from Serena. "Have some sense, man."

"Then meet me at dawn on the field of honor."

"Over my dead body," said Serena's mother from the doorway.

Serena sucked in a relieved breath. She had no chance of soothing Paul's outrage. Her mother, however, might bring some sense into this chaos.

"Lady Talbot, this isn't your concern," Paul said coldly, glaring at Giles.

Her lips flattening, Serena's mother stepped inside and shut the library door. She cast a disapproving glance at the overturned table. "If you're going to bellow your head off like a charging elephant, when I have a house full of people, it does indeed concern me."

"I don't mean to cause trouble..." Paul began, only to receive a blistering look for his pains.

"Then don't."

Giles's "Lady Talbot, I must apologize..." clashed with Paul's furious "It's a matter of honor."

Serena's mother leveled an unimpressed stare on Paul. "Losing your temper and alerting the world to scandal will damage my daughter's good name. Is that what you want, young man?"

Paul's jaw set in a stubborn line. Serena knew from old acquaintance that when his obstinacy kicked in, he was impossible to shift. "If you knew what I saw when I came into this room, you'd insist on having your daughter's honor avenged."

Serena's mother subjected the three participants in this drama to a comprehensive inspection. Serena blushed, certain that her mother had a good idea just what she and Giles had been up to before Paul's belligerent interruption. "High spirits and Christmas cheer have lured you all into being a little more uninhibited than usual. It's nothing to make a fuss about."

Just like that, she transformed potential tragedy into a mild social faux pas. Ridiculously Serena wanted to cry, even as she said a silent prayer of thanks. She'd felt sick when Paul hit Giles. She'd felt worse when the shadow of the dueling field arose.

"Mamma…" she began, but her mother gestured her to silence.

"You need to fix your dress. It seems to have caught on something."

Serena's blush heightened to fire. It had indeed caught on something. Giles's exploring fingers. But when she met her mother's gaze, to her surprise, she found not anger, but compassion.

That only made her feel worse. She deserved a

stinging rebuke. Someone needed to give her a stern lecture and remind her what she wanted out of life.

"I will, of course, leave Torver House as soon as possible." Giles stood rigidly, as though he faced a firing squad. The flesh around his eye turned purple. Tomorrow, he'd look like he'd lost a boxing match.

"Don't be silly, Giles," Serena's mother said, again with a remarkable lack of censure. "It's snowing like mad out there. You won't get ten feet from the house."

"After what he's done, you can't let this blackguard remain," Paul protested.

A repressive expression placed his masculine posturing into the same category as a toddler's tantrum. "In my house, I can offer shelter to anyone I want."

"But he…"

Under her mother's unflinching regard, Paul subsided into disgruntled silence.

"I believe it's time you returned to the great hall, Paul." She glanced across to Giles. "And, Giles, you should go downstairs to the kitchens and get some ice for that eye."

"Thank you, Lady Talbot." Giles bowed. Grimness hardened his features, and that telltale muscle jerked in his cheek. "I'll call on you tomorrow morning and make my apologies before I leave."

"No need to rush off. This is a storm in a teacup."

"My lady…" Paul sounded like he was strangling.

"Our hostess has spoken," Giles said. "There's been enough theatrics already."

"Well said, Giles," Serena's mother murmured. "If you'll both excuse me, I'd like a word with my daughter."

Serena's stomach sank into her slippers. She should have known a scolding awaited. Feeling queasy with humiliation, she prepared for what was to come. Her wanton behavior had nearly sparked a catastrophe.

As he marched out, Paul shot Giles a contemptuous glare that promised future retribution. On his way, Giles paused beside her mother. His eye had turned a virulent shade and swelled shut. It must hurt like the dickens.

"I take full blame for what happened, Lady Talbot. Serena wasn't at fault."

Serena bit back a surge of disbelieving laughter. Nobody would credit that, let alone her shrewd, suspicious mother.

And why should she? It wasn't true. Serena had leaped into Giles's arms without the slightest pretense at maidenly reluctance.

"I trust to your honor," her mother said calmly.

"Maybe you shouldn't," he muttered, his hand tightening on the doorknob.

"Don't talk nonsense." Serena's mother continued to surprise her. Perhaps she'd joined Cousin Charles in imbibing too much rum punch. "I've known you since you were a boy. You've turned into a fine man,

Giles Farraday. And you're always welcome in this house."

Serena saw Giles consider arguing, before he decided disagreeing would achieve nothing. After all, no real harm had been done, although if Paul had arrived a few minutes later, the outcome might have been different. Serena had been so lost to passion, she'd have denied Giles nothing.

"Thank you, my lady." After another bow, he was gone.

When Serena's mother directed that steady gaze upon her daughter, guilt threatened to crush her. "Does everyone know?" she asked in a subdued voice.

The idea of enduring the rest of the house party under a barrage of curious, judging eyes made Serena cringe. Although given the liberties she'd allowed Giles, she ought to be a pariah.

A hint of a wry smile curved her mother's lips. "Darling, don't take this so hard."

"Do they know?"

"No. I was leaving the hall, when I saw Paul burst in like a wounded bull. The noise from the party masked anything going on in here."

The agonizing tension drained from Serena. It was hard enough to acknowledge her own stupidity, let alone having her whole family agog at her lapse. "Why aren't you furious?"

"Because you're human. Because it's not a mortal sin to steal a kiss or two from a dashing admirer.

Because I suspect you already feel bad enough for both of us."

"I do," she mumbled, avoiding her mother's eyes.

"So let's leave it at that. Although I don't know how Giles is going to explain that black eye. By tomorrow, it will be truly spectacular."

"And Paul will be a cranky bear."

"A few setbacks might do that young fellow good. He's become too complacent."

Serena frowned. "I thought you liked Paul."

Her mother looked surprised. "I do like Paul. But he'll benefit from the occasional reminder that the entire world isn't arranged for his convenience."

"He's so angry."

"He'll get over it."

"I'm not sure."

"Come here, Serena." Smiling, her mother opened her arms. "I hate seeing you so unhappy."

For a quaking moment, Serena stared at her mother before with a smothered sob, she rushed into her embrace. When immediate warmth surrounded her, she burst into the tears that had threatened since Paul had turned an act of surpassing beauty into something dirty.

"I usually love Christmas," she sniffled into her mother's shoulder.

Her mother laughed softly. "Not this year."

"I don't understand what's wrong with me—and I

still don't know why you aren't sending me to bed without any supper."

"Do you want me to haul you over the coals? It's late, and I've got a house full of people to cater to, and what you did wasn't all that terrible in the great scheme of things."

Serena drew away and stared, puzzled, into her mother's face. "But I kissed Giles."

The smile was definitely in evidence now. "And very nice I'm sure it was."

Better than nice, but a girl couldn't tell her mother that. "Don't you care?"

"Of course I do, but you're young, and the house is overflowing with mistletoe, and spirits are high. If you can't break a few rules at Christmas, I don't know what the world's coming to." She paused as Serena struggled to make sense of her mother's astonishing tolerance. "I love your father with all my heart, but if I was twenty-one and a handsome fellow like Giles Farraday wanted to kiss me, I doubt I'd hesitate."

"Paul's the handsome one," Serena said, and wondered when that had become so unimportant.

"Oh, yes, he's handsome, too. But when I was a girl, I always had a yen for the dark, intense type."

"But Papa is—"

"The jolliest gentleman in Creation. I know. Yes, well, our first impulses don't always prove to be the best ones." Her mother drew away and passed her a handkerchief. "Now, dry your eyes and go upstairs and get some sleep. You've been fretting yourself to a shadow. Trust me, darling. Everything will work out in the end."

Serena stifled the impulse to confide the whole mess from the beginning. After all, if anyone knew of her abiding fondness for Paul, it was her poor, longsuffering mother. She'd endured countless hours of listening to Serena extol his perfections.

And what was the point of confessing her sudden, powerful penchant for Giles? It wasn't as if he'd offered her anything beyond a couple of kisses.

Anyway, after a lifetime of plotting to marry Paul, how could she trust this attraction for Giles? Mere days ago, he'd been more a stranger than a friend.

Now...

Now he wasn't a friend, and he wasn't a lover. He certainly wasn't a suitor.

A passing madness was the best way to describe her unexpected weakness for the Marquess of Hallam.

Only a fool would discard a secure future in favor of a brief affair. Especially if one were unmarried, with until now, an unblemished reputation. No, far better she scotched this passion, however hot, however bright, and stick to her plans to marry Paul.

If he could overlook tonight's sins.

The idea that he might scorn her as a light-skirt shouldn't make her feel better.

"I think...I think I'm going insane," she admitted in a low voice, mopping at her sodden cheeks.

Her mother's smile was loving. "Just follow your heart, Serena. It won't lead you astray."

But as she lay awake and troubled in bed that night—she couldn't face returning to the party—she knew her heart was too unreliable to make the right decision.

CHAPTER TWELVE

After the Christmas festivities, the house lay quiet on Boxing Day morning. Serena sat alone at breakfast, staring with heavy eyes through the closed French doors to snow-swept gardens. The outlook matched her mood. Cold. Gray. Miserable.

Her attention returned to the eggs congealing on her plate. She wasn't hungry. She should have stayed upstairs. But she'd brooded most of the night, and she'd been desperate for a change of scene.

She couldn't understand what had happened in the library. Giles had touched her, and she'd tumbled into his arms without thought for the rest of the world. Propriety. Reputation. Morality. She hadn't given a fig for any of them, compared to the heady joy of Giles's caresses.

Sighing, she shifted on her chair. She'd tried to

concentrate on the horrible aftermath and feel suitably chastened. But her wicked thoughts kept shifting back to those glorious moments, when Giles had kissed her as if he starved and his hand had stroked her naked breast.

How distressing to discover that a brazen hussy lurked beneath her respectable shell. Given her flagrant behavior, Paul might have had a lucky escape. Imagine if this wild woman emerged after they married.

She'd enjoyed everything Giles had done, until Paul spoiled it. And undoubtedly saved her virtue. She should be more grateful.

But mostly she was disappointed.

It was clear that she was unfit for decent society.

She lifted her coffee to her lips and grimaced. It was ice cold. She was rising to fetch a fresh cup when the door opened.

"Oh," she said with a dismal little squeak.

Paul looked serious and sheepish. Neither expression was characteristic. "Good morning, Serena."

"Good morning, Paul," she said warily, searching in vain for some hint of the condemnation she deserved. "I was just finishing."

He made a curiously pleading gesture. "Please… I'm sure you don't want to see me this morning. But I'd very much like to talk to you."

Probably to explain that he wouldn't be proposing. "After last night, you must hate me."

He shook his head and advanced to take the seat cornerwise to her. "You can't think I blame you."

"You should," she said frankly, sinking back into her chair. Perhaps it was best to get this over with.

"It's that swine Hallam." To her surprise, his eyes were full of remorse. "The arrogant devil even warned me that I was a fool to take you for granted."

He caught her hand. Serena waited to experience a thrill—after all, she'd spent most of her life wishing that Paul Garside would look at her as if she was the only girl in the world.

Unfortunately she felt nothing but stirring impatience.

Paul went on, before she could correct his impression that she'd been a complete innocent in last night's brouhaha. "You're a naive country maiden, and he's a rake. The ladies in London were mad for him. One click of his fingers, and he had any woman he wanted. You didn't stand a chance, my darling."

Vaguely she noticed that Paul had called her his darling. More immediate was the unwelcome image of hordes of sophisticated harpies clamoring for Giles's attention. She mightn't know those strumpets, but she'd dearly like to kill them.

"You were furious," she said in a subdued voice.

"With him. Never with you." He paused. "It was my fault. I neglected you and left you easy prey for a ravening wolf."

She bit back the impulse to tell Paul that she, not

Giles, had done most of the hunting. "You make me sound like a ninnyhammer. I went into sin with my eyes wide open."

Again Paul shook his golden head. She started to find it annoying. "That's a rake's tactic, my dear, to let you think you're making the running, when all the time he's luring you to ruin."

"You seem to know a lot about it."

His remorse deepened. "I can't lie and say I've lived a pure life, but I'm ready to put aside my bachelor ways and settle down with a good woman. You'll never have to worry about my fidelity, Serena. You've always been the one for me."

Oh, no, she knew what was coming. And she absolutely wasn't ready to hear it.

"Paul…" she began, not sure what to say. It seemed stupid to ask him to give her time, when they both knew she'd been waiting for this moment all her life.

His hand tightened, and he spoke over her. "There's no lady I esteem more than you. I believe we will be very happy together, and our families will be delighted if you do me the honor of becoming my wife."

She stared appalled at him, having no idea how to respond. He paused in clear expectation of an eager acceptance.

When she didn't speak, he frowned. "My dearest, I promise no woman will be more cherished and protected and respected."

Serena swallowed to shift the jagged rock blocking her throat. It didn't work. She swallowed again.

"Last night you caught me kissing another man." Her voice sounded rusty, as though she had a cold.

His gesture dismissed her statement. "I've already told you—it's forgotten."

She tried and failed to pull away. "I haven't forgotten."

He smiled at her, as though she was a foolish, pretty little thing who should yield to his endless masculine competence. With a shock, she realized that was how he'd always treated her. As if she needed to hold his hand to cross the road.

Once she might have accepted it—she'd been so blind with infatuation, she'd happily accept anything in exchange for a morsel of Paul's attention. But after these last tumultuous days, she came to suspect that she wasn't sweet at all. Instead she was wild and wayward, and she wanted a man who treated her as an equal, not as a fragile charge on his chivalry.

"I told you, you don't need to apologize. You were blameless in what happened. In fact, I almost commend your innocence."

This time, she managed to tug her hand from his. She hid it under the table where it clenched in her skirts. "Now that's going too far."

He cast her an uncertain glance. The first sign of uncertainty he'd shown, she realized. As far as Paul was concerned, he was tying up the loose ends on a sure thing.

"Serena, I don't want to talk about last night. I want to talk about our bright future together."

She stared hard at him. His proposal had been very pretty. But one vital ingredient was missing. This time, her voice emerged steady and decisive. "Do you love me, Paul?"

He'd reached for her hand, but now he straightened in his chair and regarded her with disquiet. She wasn't used to seeing Paul less than confident. He was much more appealing when he didn't act like the master of all he surveyed. Over the last few days, she'd noted everything about him that annoyed her. Now she recalled the qualities she liked very much.

"Of course I do."

She mistrusted his swift response. "Why?"

He looked completely baffled. "We grew up together. I was here when you took your first steps. I was your first dance partner. We've shared every Christmas. You know I love you. I love your whole family."

"That was a nice answer," she said softly, picturing herself at sixteen, starry-eyed because handsome Paul Garside led her out at her first assembly in Dorchester. She'd felt like a princess in a fairytale.

Another thing she liked about Paul was that, while on occasion his self-importance misled him, he was no fool. "Only nice?"

This time she took his hand, surprised to realize that when she'd been mad for him, she'd have hesitated to touch him. Somewhere in the last days, that particular madness had passed. "Yes, nice. I love you, too."

He brightened. "Then…"

It was her turn to shake her head. "Your presence is wrapped up in all my lovely childhood memories."

"Surely that's enough," he said. "Affection and friendship add up to a lot."

"But not to love. The sort of love a man and a woman should feel for each other when they plan to marry."

Disapproval darkened his features. "You're talking about desire."

"Partly."

"You've let Hallam's kisses turn your head."

She stared down to where their clasped hands rested on the white tablecloth. Color stung her cheeks. "If I'm in love with you, I shouldn't feel the way I do when he kisses me."

"But all your life, you wanted to marry me," he said in disbelief.

She nodded. Her pride might flinch at her pursuit being no secret, but what was the point of denying something they both knew to be true? "You were very kind when I followed you around like a puppy."

His hand firmed on hers. "I want you to follow me around for the rest of my life."

"That's the problem." Gently, she withdrew, and this time, he didn't try to stop her. "I don't want to follow the man I marry. I want to walk by his side as his equal."

"You're twisting my words."

"Perhaps."

Abruptly he stood, and the flush on his spectacular cheekbones betrayed his chagrin. "Serena, will you marry me?"

Serena felt like crying. All her life, she'd lived with one dream. Now it came true, just at the moment that she realized it had always been the wrong dream.

She made herself meet his eyes. He looked baffled and disgruntled. And disappointed. What he didn't look was hurt to the heart.

Because only real love could hurt like that.

"Thank you for asking me, Paul." A crooked smile twisted her lips. "But I'm afraid my answer must be no."

"Nothing I say will persuade you otherwise?" His blond brows lowered. "I'm happy—well, willing—to wait while you reconsider your decision. Take as long as you want. I think you're being rash and headstrong."

"Indeed I am." Her smile widened. "And you don't want a rash and headstrong bride. You want someone peaceful and sweet and conformable."

"I want you," he said stubbornly.

"No, you don't."

"But all this time—"

"I know. I've been utterly unfair. And flighty, and female, and foolish. I'm grateful and flattered that you asked me to marry you. But my answer will always be no."

For a long time, he studied her. Then he drew himself up to his full height and bowed as if to a stranger. "Very well. I believe I will return home. I have estate business waiting. I wish you a very happy new year, Serena."

His manner was severe and distant. To her regret, he was upset. Of course he was. And she could imagine his considerable vanity was stinging like blazes.

"You don't have to go, Paul," she said, wondering if he'd ever forgive her. His coldness smarted, but not enough to make her change her mind. "Mamma and Papa expect you to stay until after Twelfth Night."

"Life is full of small disappointments," he said curtly. "Now if you'll excuse me?"

Oh, Paul.

But he was entitled to his fit of the sullens. He'd expected his proposal to prosper, and why shouldn't he? Handsome Paul Garside had probably never heard a woman say no. She couldn't blame him for being put out.

"Happy new year to you, too," she murmured. "And...I'm sorry."

"So am I," he said shortly, and gave her another of those chilly little bows. "Your servant, Miss Talbot."

He turned on his heel and marched out, every line

of his body bristling with offended masculinity. Serena watched him go, then picked up her coffee. Her hand shook so badly, the cold liquid spilled all over the tablecloth.

"Oh, bother," she choked out and burst into tears.

"So this is where you're lurking." Paul leaned one brawny shoulder against the doorway to a loosebox in Sir George Talbot's opulent stables.

Giles didn't turn from where he tightened his saddle straps, but his mouth thinned in displeasure. Paul was absolutely the last person he wanted to see at this instant.

In fact, make that ever.

"You know," he said neutrally, "you're always accusing me of sneaking around, as if I have no right to be here. When I'm just as much the Talbots' guest as you are."

Out of the corner of his eye, he saw Paul wince. "Sorry, old man. Didn't mean to imply that at all."

Giles frowned at his gray's glossy flank. It would be so much easier to hate Paul Garside, if he wasn't basically a decent sort. Too full of himself, which he couldn't help when every soul in the entire world fell over themselves to adore him. But still, at heart a good man.

Giles should be glad of that. He didn't want Serena matched with a cad.

He sucked in an impatient breath—he'd intended to leave at dawn, but the weather was dangerous for his horse. He didn't much care whether it was dangerous for him. If he froze to death on the road back to London, it would save him freezing to death over the coming years, when his disappointed love turned cold and sour.

He turned abruptly. "What the devil do you want, Garside?"

"Oh, my good God," Paul gasped, retreating a couple of paces.

With a self-conscious gesture, Giles raised a hand toward his black eye without touching it. He'd quickly learned that touching it was a bad idea. "Pleased with your handiwork?"

"Yes."

Giles began to wish he'd set off into the blizzard at first light. "Go back to the house, Paul. I've no idea why you sought me out. If you're here to gloat over your forthcoming nuptials, I don't want to hear it. You'd be much better inside, celebrating with the family."

Paul straightened and spoke calmly, "There isn't any celebration."

"So you haven't asked her yet." Wondering why the world continued to torture him, Giles turned to fiddle with his saddlebags. "Are you seeing all rivals off your patch, before you stake your claim?"

"It turns out I have no claim to stake."

Giles whirled around in genuine anger. "Don't tell me you've decided against asking Serena to marry you, because of what you think you saw in the library. Anything that happened was my fault. And given how you've kicked your heels up in recent years, you're a hypocrite of the first order to begrudge her a few kisses. If you break that magnificent girl's heart by jilting her, I swear I *will* shoot you."

Paul studied him, without rising to his anger. "You really do love her."

Giles's fists curled at his sides. How he wanted to wallop Paul. "And you really are a mean bastard. You can't possibly blame Serena for last night's mess. She's as pure as a lily."

"I don't blame Serena," Paul said steadily.

After a pause while Giles waited for his friend—his former friend—to berate him once more for trying to steal his bride away, he said, "Good. Now don't you have to go away and make a proposal?"

Paul shook his princely golden head. "I've already made it."

"So go away and break out the champagne. You'll forgive me if I find myself otherwise occupied, but I'll raise a glass in your honor when I get back to London —and damn you as the luckiest man in England."

"I'm not the luckiest man in England."

Giles frowned and finally looked properly at Paul, without the gray mist of misery clouding his vision.

That statement might mean Paul no longer considered Serena a prize since she'd kissed Giles.

Or it could mean…

"I don't understand," Giles said, although perhaps he started to.

Paul didn't look like Apollo ruling the sun this morning. Instead he seemed tired and defeated. Those broad shoulders held a hint of a slump, and the blue eyes were dull.

Good God, Paul looked almost…human.

"She won't have me."

"Don't be an idiot." Giles couldn't make sense of this. "You've been her dream since she could walk."

The bitter smile curving Paul's lips made him seem suddenly older. "Apparently she's moved on to other dreams."

"Ask her again." Giles had been hurt too often to leap to conclusions. "You've made her wait. She's just repaying the favor."

"Does that sound like Serena to you? She's always been the most forthright of women. No, my friend, she refused me, and I'll wager my estate twice over that I stay refused."

"But why?"

The bitter smile lingered. "I think she's in love with someone else."

"Someone else?"

Paul sighed, and to Giles's surprise, he reached out to clap him on the shoulder with a hint of their old affection. "Love has turned you into a buffle-headed idiot, old chum. You're usually quicker on the uptake."

Giles stared speechless into Paul's face, at last reading the truth. Without a word, he shoved past the other man and set off for the house at a run.

CHAPTER THIRTEEN

"So I've found you." His heart racing, Giles burst through the high marble doorway of the summerhouse where they'd quarreled a few days ago. Since then, he felt as if he'd lived through a lifetime.

He hurtled to an abrupt stop. Serena sat hunched on the bench. However hard she tried to shrink into the shadows, he could see she'd been crying.

"I thought you'd gone," she said in a thick voice.

Late last night, he'd sent her a note, apologizing for his behavior and wishing her well. Fighting his dismay at finding her in tears, Giles brushed the snow off his shoulders. "I...changed my mind."

He'd searched for her through the house and gardens, without success. It had taken him too long to think she might be here. But now he saw her, an odd diffidence held him captive. Blurting out his love and expecting her to declare hers in return seemed as impossible as it always had.

After all, just because she didn't want to marry Paul Garside, it didn't mean she wanted to marry Giles Farraday.

She swiped at her wet cheeks with shaking hands. "You look terrible."

"Your beau has a fist like a brick."

"Does it hurt?"

Like the very devil. "It's not too bad."

She cast him a skeptical glance but to his relief, didn't pursue the subject. When he ventured a step closer, she stiffened against the wall. Damn it, she looked as likely to take to her heels as give him a minute of her time.

"Giles, I'd really rather be by myself."

He gave a dramatic shiver. "By yourself and freezing."

She didn't smile. "Please go away."

"I can't leave you here crying, Serena." Ignoring her unwelcoming manner, he crossed the tiled floor and sat beside her. "Paul told me you'd refused him."

She gave a horrified gasp. "He didn't try to hit you again?"

"No. We both acted like civilized men, instead of savage brutes."

"Thank goodness." She started to torture her soggy handkerchief. "Was he very angry with me?"

Giles settled his back against the cold stone wall

behind him. While he itched to touch her, her brittle air warned him to keep his distance. He needed to tread carefully. All his future happiness depended on the next few minutes. "I think he was hurt."

She flinched. "He was so confident I'd say yes." She stared down into her lap. "He doesn't love me."

"Are you sure?" Giles frowned. "He's always been fond of you, and he came down here all fired up to propose."

Why the devil was he defending his rival? Except that his rival had been extraordinarily gracious in defeat.

Without meeting his eyes, Serena shook her head. "Oh, he likes me, and he was convinced I'd make a good wife. But love is more than friendship and affection, however sincere."

"So you refused him because he doesn't love you?"

She sucked in an unsteady breath, and the hands clutching the handkerchief tightened until her knuckles shone white. When she spoke, her voice was so low, he had to lean closer to hear. "No, I refused him because I realized I didn't love him."

There was no real reason for Giles's heart to start turning cartwheels. Not loving Paul was no guarantee that she loved him instead. "Oh."

After a pause, Serena glanced at him. She still looked unhappy. And uncertain. "Is that all you've got to say?"

He frowned thoughtfully. "Well, what I have to say

rather depends on who you do love, if you love anyone at all."

Her gray eyes, pink-rimmed from weeping, searched his face. "I've made a complete fool of myself over Paul."

"Mmm," he said noncommittally.

"Very tactful." To his surprise, grim amusement lightened her expression. "Everyone within fifty miles seems to know I set my cap at him."

"Including Paul."

"Including Paul."

He sighed. "I'd have wagered my last shilling that you'd accept him."

She went back to twisting her handkerchief between her hands. "Is that why you were leaving?"

"Yes," he said, knowing it was a declaration of sorts. "And also because I blotted my copybook last night."

"My mother was wonderful, wasn't she? She's always liked you."

"I like her. I like your whole family."

"That's good," she said.

"It is."

A difficult silence descended. Giles stared down at the black and white tiles on the floor and wondered how to angle the conversation around to whether one particular member of Serena's family liked him. More than liked him.

Words banked up inside him. Passionate words. Crucial words. Words that could change a fellow's life forever. But they all crashed hard against the barrier of his long-held belief that she could never love him.

He straightened and told himself to seize the chance and speak his heart. Damn it, he wouldn't let his courage fail now. Whatever it cost him.

But still his throat closed tight against what he must say.

A prickling sensation made him turn his head and meet her eyes. Biting her lip, she shoved her handkerchief into her pocket and sat up straight as if making a hard choice.

"Giles," she said in a very deliberate tone. "Why did you kiss me?"

Moodily he watched the falling snow outside the door. One booted foot kicked at the floor. "Because I couldn't help myself."

A quick glance revealed her dissatisfaction with that answer. "I don't mean just last night."

"I don't either. I've wanted to kiss you for years." More than kiss her, God forgive him. "When you gave me the chance, I couldn't say no, although it broke every rule in the gentleman's code."

"The gentleman's code?" Curiosity lit her eyes, and she studied him, as though he had the answer to every question. Which was ironic when he felt so completely at sea.

With another sigh, he went back to watching the snow. "The code that says you don't cut out a friend who's set his sights on a woman. Make that double if he intends to marry the chit."

"I didn't know."

"About the gentleman's code?"

"No, that you'd always wanted to kiss me."

"Well, I did."

Another thorny silence that she eventually broke. "Do you still?"

"Still what?"

She gave a brief hiss of impatience. "Do you still want to kiss me?"

He faced her. "Of course I do."

"So why don't you?"

Shock turned him to stone. Then he shook his head. "It's more complicated than that."

Her eyes darkened with something that could be disappointment. "Because Paul's not here to be jealous?"

"Bugger Paul."

"Then why?"

His mouth turned down. "Because kisses aren't enough anymore."

"Because...you're a rake and you want to seduce me?"

His grunt of laughter contained no amusement. "I want to seduce you, but not because I'm a rake."

"Then why, Giles?" The question, raw after her earlier tears, vibrated with feeling. "We're here alone. Last night you kissed me as if you were desperate for me. Yet today, you're acting like we're strangers. Tell me what you want. You've never said, and while a girl can guess, she'd rather have it spelled out."

At last, the dam inside him broke. He heaved to his feet and glared down at her. Impassioned words tumbled from his lips, although they sounded more like an accusation than a vow of eternal fealty. "Goddamn it, Serena. I'm in love with you."

She didn't respond as though he'd delivered good news, blast it. Looking uncertain, she rose from the bench and stood in front of him as he loomed over her. "You didn't tell me."

He growled low in his throat. "Why would I tell you? You only had eyes for bloody Paul."

"Not…not this Christmas," she said faintly, her breath escaping in uneven huffs. She took a tottering step toward him and extended her hands in a pleading gesture. "Do you want to tell me again? And this time, please try not to sound as if you're challenging me to pistols at ten paces."

Giles inhaled to clear his head, and this time, his mind kicked into motion and cut a path through the tangle of confusion, self-mistrust, and turmoil. Almost too late.

He squared his shoulders and raised his chin. In his chest, the hope which had shriveled into a dry husk unfurled anew. Clearing his throat, he forced the irrevocable words past his lips. He managed to regulate his voice to something less than a roar.

"I love you, Serena. I've always loved you. You fill all my dreams."

Her eyes widened with amazement, and something that looked like exultation. After another pause, she swallowed, as if speaking posed a problem for her, too. "Giles, do you know why I said no to Paul's proposal?"

"He doesn't love you."

"Yes, that's true."

She paused, and Giles feared he must explode with suspense. He was almost sure that she loved him, although balancing on the brink of hearing her admit it was excruciating.

She bit her lip again, then spoke in a rush. "But the real reason I said no is because I realized I'm in love with another man."

His eyes narrowed on her, as hope punched him so hard in the gut, it stole his breath. "That other man had better be me."

She stepped forward and twined her arms around his neck. Her tremulous smile sat oddly with her tearstained cheeks. "Who else could it be but you?"

With shaking hands, he caught her slender waist. How he ached to kiss her. But first, he needed to hear the words. "It's your turn to say it, Serena."

She rose on her toes and kissed his lips. "I love you, Giles."

Dazzled he stared down at her, while his heart gave a mighty thud of relief and gratitude. *Thank God. Thank God. Thank God.* As elation flooded through him, he released a long exhalation that he felt he'd been holding back for ten years.

She loved him. *Serena loved him.* Impossible, unwinnable, irresistible, gorgeous Serena Talbot declared herself his. He could hardly believe it. Yet when he stared into her shining silvery eyes and saw his wonder mirrored there, he did believe it.

Serena loved him. The life he'd always wanted was his for the taking.

Unfamiliar happiness made it as difficult to speak as despair ever had. He swallowed to shift the choking ball of poignant emotion jamming his throat.

"Well, it's about time," he said huskily.

His answer made her giggle, until his ferocious kiss distracted her. He sensed her surprise at the quick shift to passion, before her hands clenched on his shoulders and she met him with open-mouthed ardor.

All coherent thought vanished in a blaze of joy and heat. And love.

Finally, love.

By the time Giles came back to the world, he was sitting on the bench with Serena on his lap and her face hidden in the curve of his shoulder. When he felt a warm dampness against his neck, he pulled away to see her face. She was rosy with happiness—apart from the tears glistening in her eyes.

"What's this? You're the most contrary creature. I thought you'd be glad."

His gentle teasing roused a radiant, if waterlogged

smile. She laid one hand against his cheek. "What a fool I am. It took me so long to see the truth."

He tilted his head to kiss her palm. "There is one thing you can do to make it up to me."

"Love you forever?"

He laughed softly, even as his heart cramped to hear her speak with such ease of the love he'd believed would never be his. "That goes without saying. Another thing."

She combed her fingers through his hair and drew him down for more breathless kisses. He wrapped her in his arms and let himself feast on her lips.

"Giles?" she murmured after a long while.

"Hmm?" He nibbled a delicious path along her neck. "Why the deuce did you choose such a chilly spot for our reconciliation?"

"I didn't know we were to have a reconciliation." To his regret, she wriggled away. "As far as I was aware, you were halfway to London, after writing me a grumpy little note that consigned me to perdition."

"I didn't," he said, appalled that she'd reacted that way to his stilted farewell.

"You did. But I forgive you." Her loving look was the sunshine that melted the last frozen reaches lingering at the edges of his soul. "You said you wanted something from me."

Before she'd kissed him to the stars and back. Still, she deserved her moment.

Very gently, he shifted her onto the bench and went

down on one knee before her. The cold of the tiled floor was like a knife, even through his breeches.

"My darling Serena, I love you with all my heart." For the first time, the declaration, so simple, so complicated, emerged freely. He caught her trembling hand. "Will you do me the great honor of agreeing to become my wife?"

"My wonderful Giles," she said in a choked voice. "I can think of nothing I'd like better."

"Sweetheart…" He surged up to fold her in his arms again, but to his astonishment, she leaped to her feet and evaded him. "What in Hades is it now? I should think a marriage proposal merits a kiss."

"More than one, but let's find somewhere warmer first." Giddy happiness rang in her laugh, and she stretched up to skim her lips across his. Before he could lure her closer, she danced away. "Somewhere with a little mistletoe for luck."

Giles caught Serena round the waist, and the sizzling kiss they shared made a mockery of the bleak winter weather. Dazed, he lifted his head and smiled down at the woman he worshipped. "You and I don't need mistletoe, my love."

EPILOGUE

Lanyon Castle, Devon, February 1821

Naked beneath his vermillion dressing gown, Giles knocked at the door leading from his dressing room to the marchioness's apartments. No marchioness had occupied these rooms in over twenty-five years. Now a glorious, golden-haired woman would bring his home alive. She'd already brought the marquess alive.

After years of yearning, at last Serena was his. He'd been hers from the first.

A smile curved his lips, as he recalled this morning's wedding. It had been a perfect winter's day, cold and crisp, with a pale sun turning the landscape to diamonds. Yet the brightest diamond of all had been

Serena Talbot, now Serena Farraday, Marchioness of Hallam.

His bride had marched up the aisle of St. Lawrence's, like a conqueror entering a vanquished city. She'd worn a simple white gown and a long lace veil scattered with pearls. Serena had been incandescent with joy, and so beautiful and regal that his heart had threatened to burst with love. And astonished gratitude that this superb creature entrusted herself to him.

It had been a perfect day in every way. Marrying Serena, not only did he claim the woman he loved, he also became part of the family that eighteen years ago had embraced a bewildered orphan boy. When he escorted her to the altar, Serena's father had looked like he'd won a kingdom in a lottery. Serena's mother had shed a few happy tears during the ceremony. She'd whispered in her new son-in-law's ear before he left Torver House that she'd always known he was the one for her daughter.

Now, his wife lay in the big bed where countless generations of Farraday brides had slept. Had any man in history been as happy as Giles was tonight? He took leave to doubt it.

During their five week engagement, Serena had preserved her virtue, if only by a whisker. His control had come near shattering so many times, during their trysts in the summerhouse. If the place hadn't been as cold as a penguin's parlor, Serena wouldn't have come to church a virgin bride.

But tonight, tonight Giles's torture ended. All those years of hopeless longing, that had turned out not to be hopeless at all, would find their consummation.

His heart pounding with anticipation, he heard her soft permission to enter the room. He opened the door and paused on the threshold.

By all that was holy, she was lovely. The breath snagged in his throat. Hunger strained on its leash, but Giles intended to spin each moment out as far as he could, to eternity if possible. The first moment was this, the sight of his bride in the bed where he meant to possess her.

Serena leaned against the carved oak bedhead, the sheets folded at her waist. Her golden hair lay loose about her shoulders, and her sheer white nightgown reminded him of the dress she'd worn when she pledged herself to him.

Her breasts pressed wantonly against the frail silk. As he watched her nipples harden, his excitement mounted.

"I'm the luckiest man in England," he murmured in a reverent tone.

Flickering candles lit the room, and a fire roared in the hearth. The golden light turned Serena into a mysterious, exotic creature. "Only in England?"

A fond laugh escaped. "Well, I can't speak for the entire world. A Mogul in Rajasthan or a mandarin in Peking might vie for the title. Although I doubt it."

Her slender hands plucked at the crisp white sheets. "It's silly to be nervous."

"Very silly." Tenderness swamped his craving to take her. He strolled across to a carved Elizabethan chest where the servants had set out wine and plates of delicacies.

She observed him with a thoughtful expression. "After all, I love it when you kiss me."

He poured two glasses of claret. "I should hope so."

"And when we had the chance, we've gone beyond kisses."

The memory of tasting her delicious nipples charged his mind with red heat. "We have."

"And I've known you most of my life."

"Yes."

"So why am I worried?"

He crossed to the bed and sat on the edge of the mattress. "Because you've never done this before." He passed her a glass and summoned every ounce of heroism he could muster. "Would you rather wait? It's been a long day, and you're tired after crossing two counties."

After the wedding breakfast, they'd traveled through a fairytale landscape of sparkling snow and trees laced with frost. When they'd arrived at Lanyon Castle, her awe at its rambling, medieval splendor had helped him view his home with kinder eyes. He'd always thought of the Farraday family seat as an uncongenial monstrosity, but from tonight, he meant to create new, happier memories here. In this house, he hoped to bring up his children and live into contented old age with his beloved wife. If the castle lacked soul now, by God, it would have a soul by the time he was done with it.

Serena frowned into her untouched wine as if she considered his offer, before she glanced up at him through her lashes. "I'm not that tired. Do you really want to wait?"

Good God, no. He'd already waited what felt like ten lifetimes. "I've wanted you for so long, another night won't make much difference."

Except it was his wedding night, and he burned for her. And the five weeks of temptation since she'd admitted she loved him had proven an excruciating mixture of rapture and frustration.

Her lush mouth curled in a wry smile. "You don't sound like you mean that."

Self-derision turned down his lips. "At least give me points for trying."

"I do." She leaned forward and kissed him. "I love you, Giles."

"I love you," he said, when she drew away to taste her wine. "Would you like me to stay?"

Surprise widened her eyes. "Where else would you go?"

"The first night in a strange bed, you might prefer to sleep alone."

Her laugh banished his scruples. "I most certainly

do not. I want to sleep with my husband." She set her glass on the night table with a purposeful gesture that belied the apprehension in her eyes. "And by sleep, I mean stay awake and discover everything you learned when you were chasing all those naughty London ladies."

Elation flooded him, along with the desire he no longer had to strangle into obedience. "You do me too much honor."

"I want this, Giles." She swept the covers back to reveal her slender body in its sheath of snowy silk. "I think I've wanted it from the first time you kissed me under the mistletoe. From that moment, I was lost."

He stood, setting his wine aside. "Serena…"

Her smile brimmed with love. "Show me, my darling."

A dizzying combination of disbelief and gratitude gripped him. All his life, he'd felt like an outsider. But Serena now invited him to join her in a warm, generous world. He shrugged the dressing gown off and let it crumple to the floor. "My pleasure."

"Heavens," she breathed, surveying his naked body with a greedy curiosity that threatened good intentions. "You're quite magnificent. What a sin it is to cover you up with clothing."

An amused grunt escaped him, despite the heat stinging his cheeks. "It's too cold to run around naked at this time of year, my love."

Still her eyes devoured him. When she licked her

lips with an appreciation both innocent and salacious, he groaned.

Her brazen gaze focused between his legs, where he was hard and ready for her. "We need to go somewhere warm. Soon."

"Italy is warm." After a week in Devon, they set sail on his yacht for three blissful months in the Mediterranean.

"I may never come home."

The playful conversation soothed her skittishness, he was glad to see. "You're making me blush," he said sardonically, and with absolute truth. "Your turn."

To his delight, she accepted the challenge with alacrity. With a grace that set his pulses stuttering, she hauled the pretty nightdress over her head and tossed it away.

She was prettier than the nightdress. Much prettier. For years, he'd pictured her naked body. But the sight of her made imagination a beggar.

Every drop of moisture dried from his mouth as all the blood in his body rushed to his loins. "I was wrong," he whispered.

Serena was blushing beautifully. Her hands fluttered up to cover herself, before she forced them down to her sides. He appreciated the unspoken trust in the action. "About what?"

"I'm not the luckiest man in England."

"You're not?"

The pudding-headed girl sounded uncertain again.

Didn't she know she was the most glorious sight in Creation?

"No." His excitement mounting, he completed a leisurely inspection of the woman he loved. "I'm the luckiest man in the entire universe. There's no question."

Her smile conveyed such pleasure, he wanted to hug her. "Thank you." She paused. "If that's true, why on earth are you standing all the way over there?"

"I'm admiring the view."

And what a view it was. Her slim, white body and high, perfect breasts. The sweet little belly above a nest of dark gold curls. Graceful legs, crossed decorously at the ankles. As if such a blatantly sensual creature could have any truck with decorum.

Her fingers clenched in the sheets, but still she didn't cover herself. "You could take a closer look."

He stepped forward and leaned one knee on the bed, looming over her. "You make me so happy," he said, moved when she tilted her face up for his kiss.

More trust. He swore on everything he held sacred that he'd prove himself worthy.

He slid one arm around her waist, loving the sensation of his skin moving on hers, and tugged her up and into his body. With his other hand, he brushed the heavy fall of hair back from her unforgettable face. For over half his life, her image had been carved in his heart, but tonight he couldn't resist studying her features as if he saw her for the first time.

"I think you should kiss me," she said shakily.

"I'm taking my time," he said, tantalizing her. And himself.

Soon he'd be unable to hold out against desire's command. But for now he lingered, etching every minute detail in his memory.

He'd been so sure he'd live out his days in solitude and disappointment. Since he'd won Serena's love, the universe had turned bright with hope.

"Giles," she said with a hint of complaint, "stop tormenting me. I've been waiting too long."

He grinned. "You know nothing about waiting."

She shot him a frown. "Are you going to make this a competition?"

He laughed and kissed her quickly. "No. Because whatever happens now, I won in the end."

"So did I." A determined light entered her eyes, and she slid her hand behind his head. "Now I want to enjoy my victory."

She stretched up to press her lips to his, and he relinquished all thought of delay. He let her draw him down until he lay over her, their bodies twining together in sublime harmony.

By the time he rolled to his side to catch a breath, he admitted that the gradual approach had served its purpose. Her response showed no hint of hesitation.

Giles rose on one elbow and set out to explore the glorious landscape of Serena's body. Those heated, rushed, frustrating interludes that punctuated their engagement had taught him a lot about what she liked. Now he intended to uncover every last carnal secret.

He cupped one luscious breast and took the beaded peak into his mouth, sucking and nipping and flicking his tongue until she writhed against the sheets. Then he paid the other breast the same attention. She tasted sweeter than wine. Her musky scent made his head reel.

Still kissing her breast, he traced designs across the dip of her stomach, venturing lower with every incursion until he tangled in the soft curls that hid her sex. Her fingers kneaded his head in a silent plea to continue. He stroked her, relishing the heat and sumptuous wetness he discovered.

Serena bucked under his caresses and bowed up to nip his shoulder. The bite delivered a spike of arousal. He lifted his head and kissed her hard, as he explored her delicate folds, inch by satiny inch. When she parted her legs to encourage him, he made an incoherent sound of satisfaction. One gentle finger penetrated her, and she clenched in immediate welcome.

"Giles?" she murmured against his lips, and he heard her surprise at this unfamiliar caress.

"You'll like it."

With purposeful rhythm, he began to stroke her. Soon she was shaking, and her hands formed claws on his shoulders. "That's...wicked."

"It is indeed," he said, testing her with two fingers.

She was so exquisitely tight. A liquid surge

rewarded him when he touched her deep inside. His thumb glanced across the hidden pearl, and she shuddered and cried out, clinging to him.

Giles rose above her, resting his weight on his elbows. She curled her arms around his back and stared up with glittering interest. "I want you."

He kissed her neck, tasting her racing pulse against his tongue. "I love you."

He'd never spoken those words to anyone before Serena. Now he couldn't say them enough. Every time he did, her expression softened in a way that made him feel like a hero. This time, it was no different.

With all the poignant tenderness in his heart, he kissed her again and shifted between her slender thighs. "Tilt your hips toward me," he murmured. "And bend your knees."

Serena had always been willful and outspoken. During today's ceremony, he'd hidden a wry smile when she promised to obey him. But now she immediately cooperated, offering herself with a lavish readiness that made his heart cramp with love.

Giles edged into her, caught between the primitive masculine urge to possess and his overwhelming need to cherish. Control won out. Just.

She shifted to take him deeper. She was trembling, and a fine sheen of sweat made her skin shine. The clasp of her body was the most glorious sensation he'd ever known. Until he tightened his hips and thrust.

She gave a ragged gasp, and her nails scored his

shoulders. The sting added piquancy to the rush of exultation.

What he did hurt. Serena bit her lip, and tears sprang to her eyes.

"My darling, forgive me," Giles muttered, pressing his hot face into her bare shoulder.

"I do," she whispered as a marvelous fullness seeped through her. She felt every breath he took, each beat of his heart.

For a long time, they lay joined and unmoving. He raised his head and kissed her with a tenderness that went a long way toward making her forget the already fading pain. Gradually her body adjusted, so when at last he shifted, she discovered a stirring pleasure.

As he pulled back, a sigh of wonder escaped her. "Do that again."

"I will." Laughter warmed his deep voice. "For the next fifty years at least."

"I mean..." She moved and delighted in the extraordinary barrage of impressions. The friction of his body. His rasping breath. The rich scent of their arousal. The warmth rising between them.

"I know what you mean, my love," he said, and to prove it, he began to pump in and out with a steady power that made her blood surge as powerfully as the tide. She thrilled to the way the muscles across his back tensed and released with every movement.

When he'd touched her so shockingly, so blissfully between the legs, she'd felt a strange, hot flutter in her belly. But that had been a mere echo of the intense response coiling inside her now. The sensation, elusive, unearthly, made her whimper.

When she tilted her hips to meet him, he made a guttural sound of approval. His eyes were blind with animal hunger, and a flush darkened his skin.

Still the spiral tightened. She could hardly bear it, but the idea of stopping was unthinkable. Gasping for air, she clenched hard around him every time he plunged into her.

The tension reached an unendurable pitch. Giles's thrusts turned wild, desperate, insistent. For a breathless instant, Serena teetered on the edge of some new world.

Then lightning zapped through her, and she was flying into space. Through the clamoring ecstasy, she heard him groan. His body jerked against hers, as he surrendered himself into her keeping.

When he slumped down onto her, Serena still quivered after that glorious release. The way he crushed her trembling body into the mattress became part of the pleasure. What an extraordinary experience. She'd had no idea.

With a surge of loving gratitude, she turned her

head and kissed one of those slashing cheekbones. "I love you, Giles."

"I love you, Serena," he said in a raw whisper. He tightened his hold and rolled to the side, taking her with him.

When he tucked her into his chest, she basked in the intimate warmth of his embrace. She might have slept. She didn't know. But when she opened her eyes, she lay sprawled against Giles in perfect peace.

While she wanted to stay like this all night, all year, something must have alerted him that she was awake. He shifted up on the pillows, his hold relaxing. "You're a miracle, my lovely Lady Hallam."

She drew back far enough to see his face. He appeared younger, more carefree, and the loneliness was at last absent from his eyes. Then and there, she vowed that she'd never let him be lonely again. "I have no words."

Amusement lit his expression. "That's not like you."

She stretched luxuriantly, delighting in the glide of her skin against his. "You've made me a new woman."

"I hope not." He kissed her briefly, but urgently. "I adored your old self."

She was sure she looked smug. She couldn't help it. "You'll adore the new me, too."

"Will I indeed?"

"Oh, yes. Because if you make me feel like this when I'm a beginner, imagine what a bit of practice will achieve."

He tilted an eyebrow. "Is that so?"

She cast him a searching glance. "Please don't tell me it was like that with all those London hussies."

To her surprise, instead of taking up her teasing, he seemed uncomfortable. "Serena, it's bad form to ask about a man's romantic past."

She frowned. "So it was romantic?"

"No," he said shortly. Tension hardened the arm around her shoulders.

"Paul was always talking about how the ladies wouldn't leave you alone."

The mention of Paul struck a discordant note. At the wedding, her former suitor had felt like a mere acquaintance, although she admired his courage in turning up to wish Giles and her well. Everyone in the congregation knew he'd hoped to marry her. Her love for Giles had swiftly revealed how childish her penchant for Paul Garside had been.

Exasperation tightened Giles's lips. "Paul has a big mouth."

She leaned on one elbow, so she could study her husband. Something happened here that she didn't understand. "Perhaps."

"You're not worried about those other women, are you?" Giles reached to twine one hand in the fall of her hair. "You must know by now that I've always been yours."

She did know that. *Except...*

He looked appalled. "By God, you are worried. Silly

widgeon. Nobody can compare to you. Nobody. Until the day I die, I'll love you with every breath I take."

His fervent declaration banished the demons of insecurity that had chosen this moment to return. But she wasn't yet prepared to let this issue go. She touched his cheek, feeling the bristle of his beard under her fingers. "It's not fair to ask you to justify your past to me—especially when I spent all those years pie-eyed over Paul."

"Not fair, but I can see you're dwelling on it. On a night when I want you to be supremely happy." His smile turned sheepish. "Very well. I may as well confess all. But I warn you, my love, that you're going to find my rakish past a letdown."

Oh, dear. That didn't sound good. "Because you were so profligate?"

"Anything but." Self-derision edged his laugh. "I'm afraid my exploits have been wildly exaggerated."

"No women at all?" Puzzled, she tried to interpret his expression. "I can't believe that."

He shrugged. "Oh, it's true that I went a little mad when I first entered society. I knew you'd never have me, so what did it matter what I did? I soon realized that I was using those women as stand-ins for the woman I really wanted. Once the pleasure was done, it always had a nasty kick. I haven't shared my bed in four years."

"So the ladies didn't pursue you?" She could hardly

credit this. But meeting his grave stare, how could she doubt him?

He took her hand and raised it to his lips for a kiss that was a beckoning whisper of bliss to come. "I suspect my lack of interest was the main attraction."

"So it really has always been me?" She knew by now that he'd loved her for years, but he was still capable of astounding her with the strength and steadfastness of his devotion.

"Always."

"I'm not worthy." A lump of emotion clogged her throat, so the words emerged as a husky murmur.

The sweetness in his kiss melted her bones. "Of course you are, my darling."

"I know I haven't loved you as long as you've loved me," she said, more choked up after that potent kiss. "But I promise I'll catch up to you."

"Now, that, my beloved, is an offer I'll gladly accept." Giles drew her close and kissed her with a passion that promised a lifetime of love and happiness to come.

ABOUT THE AUTHOR

ANNA CAMPBELL has written 10 multi award-winning historical romances for Grand Central Publishing and Avon HarperCollins, and her work is published in 22 languages. She has also written 23 bestselling independently published romances, including her series, The Dashing Widows and The Lairds Most Likely. Anna has won numerous awards for her Regency-set stories including Romantic Times Reviewers Choice, the Booksellers Best, the Golden Quill (three times), the Heart of Excellence (twice), the Write Touch, the Aspen Gold (twice) and the Australian Romance Readers Association's favorite historical romance (five times). Her books have three times been nominated for Romance Writers of America's prestigious RITA Award, and three times for Australia's Romantic Book of the Year. When she's not traveling the world seeking inspiration for her stories, Anna lives on the beautiful east coast of Australia.

Anna loves to hear from her readers. You can find her at:

Website: www.annacampbell.com

facebook.com/AnnaCampbellFans

twitter.com/AnnaCampbellOz

bookbub.com/authors/anna-campbell

goodreads.com/AnnaCampbell

ALSO BY ANNA CAMPBELL

Claiming the Courtesan

Untouched

Tempt the Devil

Captive of Sin

My Reckless Surrender

Midnight's Wild Passion

The Sons of Sin series:

Seven Nights in a Rogue's Bed

Days of Rakes and Roses

A Rake's Midnight Kiss

What a Duke Dares

A Scoundrel by Moonlight

Three Proposals and a Scandal

The Dashing Widows:

The Seduction of Lord Stone

Tempting Mr. Townsend

Winning Lord West

Pursuing Lord Pascal

Charming Sir Charles

Catching Captain Nash

Lord Garson's Bride

The Lairds Most Likely:

The Laird's Willful Lass

The Laird's Christmas Kiss

The Highlander's Lost Lady

The Highlander's Defiant Captive

The Highlander's Christmas Quest

Christmas Stories:

The Winter Wife

Her Christmas Earl

A Pirate for Christmas

Mistletoe and the Major

A Match Made in Mistletoe

The Christmas Stranger

Other Books:

These Haunted Hearts

Stranded with the Scottish Earl

offering him a fleeting Yuletide diversion? Or will this
Christmas Eve encounter spark a passion that lasts a
lifetime?

A Pirate for Christmas

Pursued by the pirate...

Bess Farrar might be an innocent village miss, but she knows
enough about the world to doubt Lord Channing's motives
when he kisses her the very day they meet. After all, local
gossip insists that before this dashing rake became an earl, he
sailed the Seven Seas as a ruthless pirate.

Bewitched by the vicar's daughter...

Until he unexpectedly inherits a title, staunchly honorable
Scotsman Rory Beaton has devoted his adventurous life to
the Royal Navy. But he sets his course for tempestuous new
waters when he meets lovely, sparkling Bess Farrar. Now this
daring mariner will do whatever it takes to convince the
spirited lassie to launch herself into his arms and set sail into
the sunset.

A Christmas marked by mayhem.

Wooing his vivacious lady, the new Earl of Channing finds
himself embroiled with matchmaking villagers, an eccentric

vicar, mistaken identities, a snowstorm, scandal, and a rascally donkey. Life at sea was never this exciting. The gallant naval captain's first landlocked Christmas promises hijinks, danger, and passion – and a breathtaking chance to win the love of a lifetime.

The Christmas Stranger

At Christmastime, a stranger crossing the threshold means good fortune...

When Josiah Hale, society's favorite aristocratic architect, stumbles upon an isolated manor house in the middle of a snowstorm, he feels like he's entered a fairytale world. And Sleeping Beauty in this secret corner of Yorkshire is lovely, vulnerable Maggie Carr, surely a princess disguised as a humble housekeeper. Is Josiah her prince – or the man who will break her heart and leave her life in ruins?

But is the stranger's arrival lucky for the girl Christmas forgot?

Maggie Carr has worked as a housekeeper at isolated Thorncroft Hall since her beloved mother died five years ago. No matter how often she tells herself she's accustomed to being poor and alone, Christmas always stirs poignant memories of a time when she had a place in the world and a family to love. But this Christmas, a handsome stranger bursts into her solitary world and makes her feel like a desirable woman. Maggie has already lost so much to cruel fate. Now as the season advances and she finds herself in thrall to the man who challenges her loneliness and turns winter nights to sultry summer, what price will this irresistible passion demand of her?

Will the Yuletide enchantment vanish with the season's decorations? Or have Maggie and her Christmas stranger discovered a magic to sustain them through a lifetime of happiness?

The Winter Wife

Will a chance meeting on Christmas Eve...

Alicia Sinclair, Countess of Kinvarra, cannot believe that fate has been so cruel as to strand her on the snowy Yorkshire moors with her estranged husband as her only hope of rescue. During their rare encounters, the arrogant earl and his countess act like hostile strangers. Now that Alicia has fallen into Kinvarra's power, will he seek revenge for her desertion? Or does the dark, passionate man she once adored have entirely different plans for his headstrong wife?

...deliver a second chance at love?

Sebastian Sinclair, Earl of Kinvarra, has spent ten wretched years regretting the mistakes he made with his young bride, but after long separation, the barriers between them are insurmountable. Until an unexpected encounter one stormy night makes him wonder if the barriers of mistrust and thwarted desire are so insurmountable after all. When winter weather traps Sebastian and his proud, lovely wife in an isolated inn, could the earl and his headstrong countess have a Christmas miracle in store?

A Christmas of confusion lies ahead! Will mistletoe magic lead the way to a happy ending?